Stanley's Aquarium

Stanley's Aquarium

Barry Faville

Auckland
Oxford University Press
Oxford   Melbourne   New York

Oxford University Press

Oxford University Press, Walton Street, Oxford OX2 6DP

OXFORD   NEW YORK   TORONTO
DELHI   BOMBAY   CALCUTTA   MADRAS   KARACHI
PETALING JAYA   SINGAPORE   HONG KONG   TOKYO
NAIROBI   DAR ES SALAAM   CAPE TOWN
MELBOURNE   AUCKLAND
and associated companies in
BERLIN   IBADAN

Oxford is a trade mark of Oxford University Press

First published 1989
© Barry Faville 1989

Published with the assistance of the Literary Fund of
the Queen Elizabeth II Arts Council of New Zealand

ISBN 0 19 558197 0

The author and publishers would like to acknowledge permission given
by the University of Kentucky Press to reproduce material from:
Fishes of Western South America, by C. H. Eigenmann and W. R. Allen (1942).

Photoset in Bembo by Typeset Graphics
and printed in Hong Kong
Published by Oxford University Press
1A Matai Road, Greenlane, Auckland 3, New Zealand

CONTENTS

CONTENTS

I
KUBLA KHAN

I do not know whether I should make this a sad story or a funny story. What interests me as I begin is that I have the power to make it either or neither, and no one will ever know what I have transformed or hidden.

I still remember the moment when I discovered that words could be user-friendly. (Now at least you know that I belong to that generation who have spent a couple of school periods a week at a computer keyboard. Don't ever warn me that the chips are down. Your explanation might date you and confuse me.)

My discovery about words came during an English period when I was in the fourth form. Mrs Pendleton had told us to browse through an assortment of poetry anthologies to find some poems that we might enjoy reading. By the time I reached the table, the books with photographs and Technicolour covers had been snatched and I returned to my desk with a volume whose chafed, solid green cover spoke of many years' service to education. Its title also told me that it had not been designed for the contemporary market: *A Book of Poetry*. Not what you would call a snappy beginning for your schoolgirl of the 1980s, especially when her legs were being scoured by a heavyweight winter pinafore, plucked from the wardrobe that morning for its first outing of the year.

Slumping in my chair I idly flipped the pages, and at once realized that I had stumbled upon a small piece of educational history. Confronting me were two decades of intellectual droppings. Poem after poem was framed by scribbled notes, some faintly pencilled, others in an arrogant ball-point scrawl. I guessed that the pencilled offerings pre-dated those written in blue,

1

black, red, and green ink. They seemed more surreptitious, as though the scribe had been ashamed of defiling the virginal white margins. Besides, pencils were becoming rare implements in my time. A demand for something to be written in pencil usually produced a storm of borrowing requests around the room. Our weapon was the ball-point, available in a range of colours to suit all moods and occasions, with the felt-tip marker as a back-up when you really wanted the graffiti to stay put.

The other clue in dating the array of annotations lay in the messages themselves. Invariably the less subtle reactions such as, 'A load of crap!' or 'This poem sucks!' were written in ink. But then, so were the notes that caught my eye. They were printed in a neat, carefully formed, bright purple script. They squirmed for space alongside the opening stanza of 'Kubla Khan: Or A Vision in a Dream', by Samuel Taylor Coleridge (1772-1834).

> *In Xanadu did Kubla Khan*
> *A stately pleasure-dome decree:*
> *Where Alph, the sacred river, ran*
> *Through caverns measureless to man*
> *Down to a sunless sea.*

Alongside I read: 'Note musical qualities: rhyme word at end of line linked by alliteration to one of the words just before it. e.g. *K*ubla *K*han; *d*ome *d*ecree; *r*iver *r*an; *m*easureless to *m*an; *s*unless *s*ea.'

It was obviously a note dictated by a teacher, presumably intended for someone's notes, but had found its resting place on the text instead. I was not struck blind by any sudden revelation about the poem's inner meaning. What caught my interest was the realization that Samuel Taylor had sat down and cold-bloodedly put those words just where he had wanted them. They had let him push them around. There had been no flash of inspiration from a friendly Muse. Samuel Taylor had made the decisions and he had pushed and prodded until the stanza had clicked into place. If you could do that with words, you could do it with paint or stone — or your thoughts.

(Naturally there are those among you who will smugly point out that Coleridge claimed the poem sprang fresh, ready-made, from his mind after he awoke from a deep sleep induced by a heavy night on the opium. Personally, I don't believe it. Pure public relations to sell the poem if you ask me. And if it was true, it was his mind that made it up anyway.)

I took the book home with me, slipping it into my bag at the end of the period. Mrs Pendleton never bothered counting back the books that she had wrenched in haste from the top cupboard — only the stuff she had borrowed from the Resource Centre, where cards and booking plans had to be filled out. Described in this way I suppose my discovery seems trivial, but it was the timing of the moment that was crucial for me. On that particular day I was miserable. I was wallowing. Someone had pushed me out too deep.

The girls I knew at school were not close friends, but we moved together as a tribe and whispered secrets like ritual chants that bound us loosely to each other. In the fourth form we whispered about boys, preferably boys who were older than we were. We passed notes to each other in class. An open grin from a fourth form boy rated no mention whatever; a smile from a fifth former was recorded with glee; to be looked at by a sixth former warranted a paragraph; and a sideways glance from a seventh former could inspire a page, especially if he hadn't shaved for a few days. Faded jeans and chin stubble were very fashionable then.

3

For my part, I joined in these games much as I had learned to play hopscotch or twirl a skipping rope when I had been younger, not because I especially wanted to, but simply because it was the thing to do. The fourth form game was no different until the moment Coleridge showed me how to be a word-user, which was the day after I had my first encounter with Duncan McDonald. He was in the fifth form. His younger sister, Angela, was in my class. One day a few of us were standing around on the lower field swapping compliments. Today's target was Dunkie — the pimply, gangly, socks-around-the-ankles Duncan, who had just broken out with a new tinted streak in his lank hair.

'He's neat!' said one.

'He's ace!' said another.

'Angela says he's a knob,' I observed.

The others looked at me. 'She would, wouldn't she? He's her brother. What do you reckon about him?'

'Oh, I think he's fantastic! Really fantastic,' I gushed. At that moment the man himself sauntered by and leered in our direction.

'He smiled at you!'

'Did you see that? He did! He smiled right at you, Robbie.'

Personally, I would have called it a recognition signal from a passing primate, but I would have sacrificed my tongue rather than admit it. Saving face was not a Chinese invention; they merely elevated it to an art form. So I smirked and looked mysterious.

I quickly forgot the incident, but my acquaintances did not. I discovered only later what happened next. Apparently Angela learned of her brother's impulsive snigger and decided that it was the symptom of feelings he was too embarrassed to express, and that the object of this suppressed affection was me. It could have been anyone. Angela had decided that romance was missing from her brother's life and that she should help him emerge from his shell. Or she could have decided that the opportunity to make a little mischief was too good to miss.

Anyway, soon afterwards Duncan began to find mysterious notes appearing in his school bag. Or a piece of folded paper would fall out of his pencil case. They all said the same thing: 'Robyn says she likes you'; 'Robyn says she thinks you're fantastic, but she's too shy to tell you'; 'Robyn wants to meet you after school'.

Of course, Dunkie's razor-sharp mind immediately went to his sister. Although the handwriting looked unfamiliar, he carefully checked it against one of Angela's exercise books when he thought she wasn't looking. She was. I learned all this later from the accomplice Angela had enlisted to be her scribe, while she dictated the messages.

I knew nothing of this at the time, though for a couple of days I had detected a strangeness in Duncan's behaviour in the playground. In a school as small as ours the knots of pupils that idled about the grounds like groups of browsing animals invariably noticed each other as they strolled by. When I observed Duncan hastening past my companions and me with averted eyes, and starting loud conversations with one of his mates as they approached, I knew that something had happened to panic the herd. I never imagined that I was the cause, until the afternoon before my encounter with 'Kubla Khan'.

It was an appropriately bleak day with the first cold southerly of the year scratching and clawing its way across the lake, speckling its grey surface with white. I had to walk against it for much of the way home and I made a mental note to move into winter uniform next day. I noticed someone loitering around the end of my street. He was some distance off, but I saw him start and begin walking rapidly in my direction. Then he deliberately slowed to a saunter, as though he was strolling nowhere in particular and the crossing of our paths when it happened would seem pure coincidence.

(This analysis is not fanciful. I know. I was born with the gift and I know it will hang from my neck like a demon's curse haunting me until the day I die. I cannot stop myself probing beneath the surface of things. If you do not understand what I mean by that, think yourself lucky! It wasn't until I read *Hamlet* that I found comfort. I also thought the ghost of Hamlet's father was a prize bastard who should have kept his problems to himself.)

The sauntering youth was Duncan. He pretended not to notice my approach. Then he uttered a strange guffaw and gave a jerky wave. His face was pink. A couple of paces past me he stopped. He spoke, as though he had just remembered something at that precise moment.

'Oh, gidday, you're Robbie aren't you? Robyn Kemp?'

I paused, facing him, and nodded.

'Lucky I bumped into you,' he mumbled. 'Been something I wanted to mention.'

'What's that?' I could feel my face growing as red as his.

'Nothing much — well, look, it's these notes. I mean it's no good. I'm with Sally,' he blurted. 'You know what I mean?'

I gaped at him and my silence heightened his confusion.

'I mean, I know you go for me, but it's no good — I've got Sally. I thought I ought to tell you. I thought it's the proper thing to do.'

Still I said nothing, and in his anxiety to clear the air his words grew crystal hard. 'So lay off the notes

6

will you? It's just no good, because I've got Sally and you're just a . . .'

He broke off because I turned away and began walking. I heard him walking too, then breaking into a run. If he had glanced back he would have seen me with my head lowered, brushing my hand across my face. He would have thought I was heart-broken because that would have fitted the scene he was playing.

But I felt as I had the day, years ago, when I had been suddenly slapped in the face at pre-school by a child I had never seen before. (Apparently I had picked up a building block to which she had established sole rights.) I was simply shocked into a stumbling walk. Then came the realization that there had been some dirty work afoot, that some of my sisters in romance had been taking my name and feelings in vain and papering Dunkie's belongings with my protestations of love.

But what really made a couple of tears jump to my cheeks, and my blood run hot with embarrassment and humiliation, was that suddenly I felt sorry for Duncan — and all that was too much to handle at once. He was doing the honourable thing. 'I thought I ought to tell you,' he had said. He could have cut me down at school at any time he chose, but he had planned an encounter and done his best. It wasn't his fault that he had bumbled his lines. He had simply delivered his speech to the wrong leading lady. So there I had the truth, clickety-click, in my remorseless little brain, and comfort had I none! Nothing! I had figured out everything and I ended up feeling miserable.

Then the following morning the opening lines from 'Kubla Khan' entered my conscious mind and I knew with certainty that I felt better. Perhaps the image of the sunless sea soaked up for me all I had felt while staring at the cold lake the afternoon before.

What really got to me was how cunningly old Coleridge had done it, how he had made something, knowing that his words would bewitch a reader with their sounds and all because he had decided they would. He considered the possibilities and slid the words around, then fixed them on the page like monuments. Only he knew, and would ever know, what he could have done instead. Perhaps I was trying to see myself as a damsel with a dulcimer singing of Mount Abora. At the time I merely knew that I had stumbled upon a part of me where I could be safe from the world, where I could think of myself in my own language and never again have to bother about the utterances of others. Of course, I did not realize then that there would be a price to pay for this kind of personal peace.

At morning interval Angela said to me, 'Duncan told me about yesterday.'

'What about it?'

'You know — what he told you. He said he told you he didn't like you.'

'He told you he told me he didn't like me? He told you that?' The conversation was becoming insane. All these 'tolds' were making me think of bells in a cathedral, and I giggled.

Angela was irate. 'Don't you care?'

The day before a question like that would have had me scurrying back onside at once. I would have cared like anything because it would have been expected of me because I belonged to the tribe. But I couldn't be bothered. I just shrugged. Angela stomped off seeking sympathetic ears. Then who should wander into sight but Dunkie. He was glancing at me. He expected me to lower my head and look the other way. But I didn't. I stared directly at him as he passed — and I winked. He nearly tripped over himself as he disappeared with his mates around the corner of the building.

I felt great. I also felt the faintest twinge of loneliness, or rather the state of being alone, which is not quite the same thing. But I muttered to myself, 'beware her flashing eyes and floating hair', and wandered off to find Angela's closest friend. I wanted to find out exactly how Angela had set me up, not that I needed much telling. But it's always worth knowing these things.

II
PUMICE

As I grew older I came to think of Taupo as being born from pumice and doomed to return to it, perhaps sooner than it imagined. Sprawled on the edge of the craters from which the lava had boiled, foaming and seething, the town spread itself over pumice like a coloured quilt, growing greener year by year, edging hesitantly around the shores of the lake, a subdivision at a time.

My father carved small statues from pumice in the workshop at the back of the garage. He would sit, a mask around his nose and mouth, gently cutting, scraping, and rubbing. From the large blocks of soft pumice strange shapes would emerge. He favoured mythical beasts — serpents or dragons — or he would carve heads like masks with long rectangular noses and high foreheads which he set up in the garden.

'Why do you put them in the garden?' I once asked him.

'Because I don't like gnomes fishing from toadstools,' he said.

My father is a draughtsman. He is a gentle man. He says little. As far as I know he is contented, ruling up plans day after day at his drawing board, sometimes designing a small building or home extension. When I was a small child I had always taken his hobby for granted, but as I grew older I noticed that he always spent more time in his small workshop when he was anxious, or when times were stressful. He would sit with pumice dust floating around him and I came to think that I could sense nostalgia in him as he quietly worked. A feeling that he was seeing something that might have been, but which was now out of reach beyond a slammed door — something that constantly itched as he scraped and rubbed and gouged at it. Or maybe he just enjoyed knocking blocks of pumice around.

My mother kept small pieces of pumice in every room in the house where water was laid on, ready and waiting in case you wanted to rub a stain from your skin. She used to wander along the beach whenever we went for a swim or a barbecue searching for small pieces of pumice, as near spherical as possible.

'Why do they have to be round?' I once asked her. 'They keep rolling away and ending up behind the door or somewhere.'

'Because round ones are nice,' she replied, 'and anyway, I don't mind if they want to move around occasionally.'

When I was in the sixth form I had a job in a chemist's shop, working after school for a couple of hours, three afternoons a week. I was amazed to discover a basket of pumice standing near the counter. Pinned to the container was a sign which read: Nature's Answer to Ingrained Grime and Dirt. Fifty Cents.

Two days passed before I found the courage to ask my new employer the reason for what seemed the biggest rip-off of all time. 'People can walk down to the lake shore and pick up the stuff absolutely free,' I said.

'I know. I've been telling customers that for years — mostly tourists. They come in wanting top quality pumice. They won't believe me when I tell them to take a five minute walk down to the lake front. They only want the best, top quality stuff.'

'So you give them what they want?'

'I have to. Every month or so I go down to the lake front, fill a sack with pumice and sell it off.'

'Even so, fifty cents?'

'I started at ten cents. People asked me if I had something better. I went up to twenty cents, then fifty. That's when the sales boomed. Mind you, I give each piece a good wash first.'

I gave up my job at the chemist after two or three months. I disliked the regular hours, the repetition of the work, and the endless trail of people handing prescriptions over the counter. There was one old man in particular who came in every week, always when I was there. His face was forlorn when I first saw him. On each succeeding visit his grey skin seemed to have settled deeper on to his cheek bones and his eyes were sucked further into their shadowy sockets. He was slowly dying. When I noticed that his doctor had abruptly increased the strength of the tranquilizer he was prescribing, I knew I had to get out of there before the old man stopped coming in.

When I told my father he said, 'Why don't you find a job mowing lawns?'

I shrugged. 'I'd never thought of that.'

'Why not? You're good at mowing lawns. Doing the lawns for two or three people would give you all the pocket money you need.'

The idea appealed to me at once. I had been cutting the grass and trimming the edges around our place since I was twelve or thirteen years old. My father trained me to do it in a way that startled me at the time. I remember that morning vividly. It was a Saturday and I was lying on my unmade bed reading a book. He suddenly appeared beside me in my room without first knocking at the door. That was unusual in itself. He seemed tense.

'I want you,' he said.

'What for?' He was upset about something and my

first thought was that I had committed some dreadful sin.

'Don't argue, Robyn.'

His calling me Robyn instead of Robbie did not reassure me and I feared the worst. He led me outside, down to the garden shed. The rotary mower was on the lawn. He didn't look at me. He just started talking as though he had rehearsed his lines, speaking to me as though I were a stranger.

'Before you start, always check the oil level and top up the petrol tank. The petrol is in that can there. Tell me whenever it gets low. You fill the tank using the funnel. Always tip up the can with the opening nearest you, otherwise you'll spill fuel over the edge.'

He showed me, then made me do it. He took me through the whole procedure of adjusting the blade height, placing the catcher in position, starting the engine, and then instructed me on how to cut the grass — how to go around trees, how to mow along the edges of the paths, how to empty the catcher. He watched me until I had more than half finished the lawn, correcting me every time I slipped up.

Then he said, 'That's how you mow the lawns. I want you to do them every week when they're growing fast.'

He turned and walked away, leaving me to finish. I thought he made a choking noise as he went, but I could not be sure I heard properly through the sound of the engine. I watched him go, feeling confused. As he passed the corner of the house to walk down to the garage I noticed the curtains twitch at the lounge window. My mother was standing there. Her eyes were filled with tears. She was watching my father with an expression of such sadness that I felt my own eyes beginning to prickle. She glanced up at me and smiled gently. The misery seemed to drain out of her. She grinned, pulled the curtains back to their fullest extent with a fierce jerk, then motioned me to get on with it. I was now feeling *very* confused.

Neither of them said very much for the rest of the day. Everything appeared to be normal and I kept to myself. That evening my mother came into my room to put some ironed clothes away in my dressing table. I was slouched on my bed, reading as usual. She hesitated before leaving the room, then sat beside me.

'Mowing the lawns,' she said, 'was always going to be Robert's job. Dad always used to talk about Robert mowing the lawns when he was old enough.'

I glanced at her and said impulsively, 'Then I suppose it means that he thinks I'm all right after all.'

I blurted it out hardly aware of what I was suggesting. She leaned over quickly and clumsily hugged me. 'You know more than I ever imagined,' she whispered, then she left the room.

That was one of the first times that I can clearly remember sensing what was happening inside someone else's mind — I mean things other than those that you can see revealed on people's faces. I have no memory of Robert. If he had lived he would have been my elder by two years. He was killed on the road, knocked down by a car when he suddenly darted from the footpath. I knew him only from a few photographs, a pudgy two-year-old grinning for the camera.

The events of that day made me understand better my life with my father until that time. He had always been affectionate towards me, treating me almost like a doll, but always seeming to stop short of loving me. As I worked it over in my mind, I decided that something must have happened that day to make him shift aside his memories of my dead brother and allow me to become fully part of him. I never found out what caused it. It must have been something he wanted to do — something he achieved with a kind of grim effort, finally stamping out a burning ember inside him.

A few days later he asked me to help him sand down a head he had been carving from a particularly beautiful piece of white pumice, streaked here and there with brown and pink. It was the first time he had ever asked me to assist him. The head was of a young man, quite different from his usual carvings. When it was finished he did not install it in the garden with the other pieces, but placed it on the top of the bookcase in the living-room where he could look at it. When I was older I fancied that I had been witnessing the final wrenches and aches springing from deep-seated grief. As a final clue I offer the fact that after that time my father never again called me Robyn, always Robbie.

Mowing lawns, my father said. Why not? I thought first of approaching a few of our neighbours, though most of them appeared to have at least one hale and hearty specimen who enjoyed the job. At weekends our neighbourhood sounded like a test bench for two- and four-stroke engines.

As it happened, I searched no further than the classified ads in that day's edition of the *Taupo Times*. There it was: 'Boy wanted to mow lawns and help with gardening.' There was an address given in a part of town where the price of homes and the size of the sections went together with genteel, elderly people long since retired, living off the spoils of their pension schemes or inheritances. Prospective applicants were invited to apply personally to be looked over. The fact that I did not qualify on the first count did not bother me in the least. I have never been a strong advocate of the 'girls can do anything' theme, mainly because I can think of a great number of things I don't want boys to give up doing, but when the occasion requires I can stand up for my rights with the best of them.

15

So I set off next afternoon on my trusty ten-speed to meet the man who wanted his lawns mown. I've enjoyed riding a cycle for several years now. In fact it was something I took up soon after I was trained to use the mower. (There, I suppose, is another clue. My father gave me my first ten-speed as an unseasonal gift, it being neither Christmas nor my birthday.) I rode to the address and swept up to the gate, ready to battle if need be with anyone who doubted my abilities. And that was when I met Stanley Swinton and began the most bizarre experiences of my life so far.

III
STANLEY

The house was set close to the road and almost filled the front of the section. On one side a cobble-stoned drive filled the space to the neighbour's fence and ran to a garage; on the other side a mass of shrubs screened whatever view there might have been of the rear of the section.

I propped my bike against one of the huge tubs that lined the wall of the house on the edge of the drive. From each of them grew a shrub, carefully tended with hardly a dead leaf in sight. I noticed that tubs and planters extended round the front of the house, some of them resting on a broad pebble garden full of carefully raked scoria that spilled from the front base boards. What lawn there was between it and the front fence could have been mown in minutes. I wondered what lay to the rear of the house. The mowing job certainly had little to do with the front.

I knocked at the door and waited. It was opened by a small plump woman wearing a kind of poncho knitted in the most brilliant colours in rectangular patterns, slashed across a dark red background. She was carrying some knitting and held a pair of rimless spectacles in her other hand. Her greying hair was cut short and combed straight with a fringe which swept to one side above a sweet, gentle, smiling face. She looked so quaint in the exotic garment she was wearing that she reminded me of something out of *The Hobbit*. I resisted the temptation to check her feet for fur.

'Can I help you, dear?'

'I've come about the job.'

'The job?'

'There was an ad in last night's paper asking for

someone to mow the lawns.'

'Of course, that was Stanley.' She looked concerned. 'But I think he wanted a boy. He's seen several boys this afternoon.'

As if on cue, a deep booming voice sounded from inside the house. 'Is that someone else who's come about the job, Elizabeth?'

Elizabeth glanced at me, then stared more closely. I stared back. She winked. 'Yes, Stanley, it's another applicant.' Then she whispered, 'Don't let him put you off dear.'

She moved away from the door and I heard footsteps approaching. A glimpse of white hair at the end of the hallway made me wonder briefly if I was about to see Gandalf reincarnated, but Stanley Swinton, though tall, was no magician. His white hair was cropped almost to crew-cut length and his face was not one that suggested hidden mysteries (which just goes to show how dangerous it is to rely on first impressions and outward appearances).

His skin was brown, permanently tanned, and dotted with deep pores, especially on his nose. This man, I thought to myself, has sweated mightily and will sweat again come high summer. But there were other marks. Scars — small pits faintly white under the tan — spread right across his forehead with a few scattered on his cheekbones and nose. Put like this his face would seem to be a gruesome mess, but in fact the effect was like that of an ancient, eroded landscape — dignified and resilient and full of hard experience.

His lips were thin and leathery. They suddenly parted in a grin to reveal an immense gold filling in one of his front teeth. 'My face seems to fascinate you,' he said. 'I once caught smallpox, many years ago. What you see are the remains.'

'Oh no, not at all,' I gulped, thinking quickly. I hate

being caught staring at people. 'Actually, I was admiring your filling. It looks fantastic — gleaming in the light — I've never seen such a big one —'

'Were you indeed? My golden tooth attracts you does it? That's interesting.' And he was interested too. His eyes appeared to brighten and he stared at me a little longer than I thought absolutely necessary.

'I didn't know you could catch smallpox in New Zealand.'

'It's most unusual these days,' he said, 'though I didn't pick it up here.'

'Whereabouts then?' I asked.

'You're an inquisitive young miss aren't you? If you must know, I was afflicted in South America, long before you were born. As you can see, I recovered. But now you had better tell me why you're here. I presume you haven't come just to admire my gold filling.'

'I've come about the job.'

'The job? I advertised for a boy.'

This was it. I had to decide on my strategy. I had a strong hunch that arguing the feminist cause with sweet reasonableness would get me nowhere with this character. He had the look of a man who enjoyed testing people, just as a virulent disease had tested him and surrendered, leaving behind a few mementoes in his skin.

'I know you advertised for a boy, but I think that was silly.'

Mr Swinton raised his eyebrows. 'Why?'

'Because I think you should employ someone who knows how to mow lawns.'

'How would I know that?'

'Try me out. Did you try out the others?'

'I must admit I did not. They seemed more interested in finding out what I was going to pay.'

From the touch of scorn in his voice I knew I was

scoring points. 'Well, why don't you let me mow a few strips for you?'

This time he smiled faintly. 'I think that's a splendid idea,' he said. 'Follow me.'

He stepped past me and led the way to the side door of the garage. I had time to notice a gleaming car in the half-light before he ushered me towards the rear door. 'I keep the mower up at the end of the garage.' He opened the back door and, as the light poured in, I saw to my relief a mower exactly like ours parked just inside.

'Why don't you wheel it out and see if you can get it started?'

OK you wonderful, patronizing old bastard, I thought to myself. I assumed an expression of utter nonchalance and wheeled the machine into the sunlight. I found myself in another enclosure, carpeted in thick, lush lawn with a tall hedge screening the back of the section. I removed the petrol cap in a series of commanding twirls. I saw that the tank was half full. The cap on the oil sump wondered what had hit it as I spun it free. I glared at the dipstick, replaced it, then screwed the cap tight.

'Four-stroke engine,' I muttered, as if I had never seen one before. I set the throttle to 'start' and prepared to fire the engine. 'Do you want me to use the catcher?' I inquired innocently.

'Perhaps you'd better,' he said. His eyes twinkled and I knew that he was impressed by my performance as much as my display of knowledge. 'Allow me.'

He brought out the catcher. I slipped it into place, started the engine and looked at him inquiringly.

'Just mow up and down here,' he said, pointing to the grassed alley-way.

I mowed three or four strips down to size, taking special care with the edge of the path that ran alongside the lawn. Then Mr Swinton looked towards the open lawn beyond the jutting hedge that obscured the remainder of the property. 'Try around that tree.' He pointed towards a small rimu growing alone.

I noticed that the grass at the base of the trunk had been carefully clipped and I knew that my prospective employer was proud of his garden — just how proud I was soon to discover. I eased the cutting edge of the blade carefully around the tree, shaving a circle of grass around the trunk. Then I waited. Mr Swinton sauntered over and switched off the engine. 'Do you think you could handle the rest of it?' he said, waving to the rear of the section.

I had been concentrating so hard on passing my driving test that I hadn't even glanced down the back. When I did I drew my breath in sharply. I had been expecting your standard New Zealand back lawn with a clothes-line, a few fruit trees, and a vegetable garden somewhere near the back fence. What I saw was a small forest of shrubs and trees that seemed to stretch towards the horizon. When we walked towards it I saw that Stanley Swinton had created an illusion. The ground sloped in graceful undulations, moulded into hillocks and shallow hollows. Narrow avenues of lawn wound and looped among small islands of shrubs and low spreading trees, many of them rhododendrons and all of them evergreen. The trees grew taller the further we walked and I saw the reason for the illusion of vastness.

The eye was carried along the tops of the shrubs and trees at a slowly climbing angle and when it reached the outer limit it did not want to stop. When you stood in the middle of the maze you could see nothing but foliage. The sounds of the street were smothered in the endless hum of insects and the chatter of small birds. There were bird feeding stations attached to many of the trees and lumps of fat hanging from branches. On others, small cups which must have held honey or some kind of nectar were surrounded by orbiting insects and even the occasional butterfly.

All this was girdled by a tall fence of ponga trunks lashed together by wire, though the sprays of small fronds growing from them camouflaged the way the fence had been built. It looked like a dark wall growing out of the ground. Yet all this had been cultivated in an area not much larger than a generous town section.

'I never imagined anything like this could exist,' I said. 'It must have taken you years to grow.'

'Not so many years,' Mr Swinton replied, 'if you know what to plant and how to grow it.'

'But why — why did you —'

'Because I've always wanted a forest of my own,' he said. 'My very own civilized jungle.'

Then I noticed a small building nestled against a side fence. Painted green and brown, it was barely noticeable until you were close to it. Steam escaped from a concrete box adjacent to the door which made me think of a heated greenhouse, except that there wasn't a pane of glass anywhere in its construction apart from a couple of skylights.

'You have a thermal bore,' I said. 'Is it a kind of hothouse?'

'No, it's not a hothouse. I keep an aquarium. I'm very fond of breeding fish.'

'Could I have a look?'

'Not just now — the temperature inside is affected if you open the door too much. In fact, I want you to stay away from there. I like to keep it isolated, in a kind of quarantine. Do you understand?'

'Of course,' I said. 'If you're breeding valuable goldfish you wouldn't want them disturbed would you?' Then the implication of what he had said sank in. 'You want me to stay away from there. Does that mean I've got the job?'

'I suppose it does.' He touched me lightly on the head. 'I think you'll do very nicely. There's not much to do — just mow the strips of lawn around the trees. But I want them tended properly and you strike me as being a careful person. Would ten dollars a week suit you?'

'That would be fine,' I said.

'Once a week then, whenever it suits you. The mower and the other gardening gear are stored in the garage. When would you like to start?'

'Right now if you like.'

'Let's leave it until tomorrow. It's getting late and there'll be dew on the grass soon.'

As we wound our way back up the lawn the shadows were lengthening. We walked down the other side of the house, away from the drive. It was like emerging back into suburbia after a week in a far-away forest. Approaching the front, I could hear the noise of traffic again. The fence slowly sank to waist level and the grounds reverted to something that resembled a photograph in a home-maker's magazine. From the front of the house I could see that the Swintons had a panoramic view of the lake. The setting sun lit up the high snow on Ruapehu and Ngauruhoe and cast shadows across the whole frame of mountains and hills that spread in an arc around Turangi. It was one of those still late afternoons when the lake is as calm and flat as a postcard, without a rumple or a torn corner to be seen anywhere. I could see four or five launches sliding slowly back and forth off Rangatira Point trolling on the evening rise, and one of the commercial launches much further out steering for the Western Bay. It was a moment made for clichés and when Stanley Swinton spoke I expected one of the standard comments about the grandeur of the view.

But instead he said, 'You are looking at one of the most dangerous places on the face of the earth.'

He said it without a trace of irony or humour. I was so startled I couldn't think of a single thing to say, not because I found his remark outlandish, but because I had never imagined that another living soul felt the same way about Lake Taupo as I did. I regarded it as a private vision, and its sudden invasion came as such a shock that all I could do was mutter thanks for the job and promise to get to work as soon as possible.

I pedalled home feeling very puzzled. I was delighted to find myself gainfully employed so quickly, but even more rapt with the discovery that my employer promised much in the way of new and interesting experiences. What puzzled me was where a man like Stanley Swinton could possibly have come from. He was more of a mystery than I had first imagined. When I reached home I announced the news of my successful expedition to the Swintons and my father said, 'I knew you could do it. What did he say when he saw you were a girl?'

'I gave him a demonstration he couldn't resist.'

'You what?'

'I mowed a strip or two.'

My father chuckled. 'What's he like?'

I described Mr and Mrs Swinton, their house and their amazing forested garden and asked him if he knew anything about them. He had heard the name, but not much more. He seemed to recall someone mentioning that the Swintons had travelled a great deal, but as far as he knew they had moved to Taupo after Mr Swinton retired. Retirement is the town's number one growth industry.

'Mrs Swinton spins and knits,' called my mother. She was in the kitchen stir-frying in two woks at once, which makes a noise like a roomful of spitting cats warming up for mortal combat. But my mother has always had the apparent ability to hear what anyone says, no matter where she is in the house.

'She does what?' I shouted.

'She spins and knits. I remember seeing something she had done in a craft display a few months ago.'

That explained the magnificent garment Mrs Swinton had been wearing. I looked forward to my future dealings with the Swintons. But my first couple of visits passed perfectly normally, partly because Mr Swinton seemed to be away. (His wife simply said hallo on my arrival and waved goodbye when I had finished mowing the lawns.) And anyway my mind was on other things because the start of my new job coincided with my re-acquainting myself with Duncan McDonald — dear old Dunkie of my fourth form days.

IV
DUNKIE

At assembly in the school hall the sixth formers sat together near the rear on the left-hand side, one year away from the ultimate — the seventh form rows at the back, whose occupants had discarded school uniform for ever and were permitted to wear normal clothes. The older we grew the more the restrictions of uniform chafed, and many found a hobby in testing the limits of the regulations. What, after all, was sensible footwear? Define an acceptable windproof jacket if you can. Personally, I found the whole game rather tiresome. I noticed that as soon as one rebel got away with something the whole mob imitated the miscreant so that you ended up with more rebels than conformists.

The other variation in the game was to clad yourself completely in all the required items of uniform, but to wear them in a way that made it clear you did so under sufferance. At that time many boys of a certain age took to wearing the tails of their grey uniform shirts hanging over their trousers like wayward aprons. Some signal triggered the fashion, as mysterious as the one that is supposed to send lemmings waterfalling over cliff tops, and something just as unfathomable made boys decide to tuck their shirts in again when they grew older.

Dunkie reached this milestone when he moved into the seventh form, and I was in my sixth form year. His face grew into its adult contours, his hair glowed darkly with shampoo gloss and his voice began to rumble steadily — all the time. All this had not escaped my attention. In the sixth and seventh forms we were thrown together in the senior common-room where we gathered at morning interval and at lunch-time to drink tea and coffee from polystyrene cups and socialize in splendid isolation, away from the great exercise yard of the playground. It was a time when the past could be forgotten, or clung to, where old cliques could dissolve and new ones form, and a greater sense of togetherness could be felt.

So I accepted it as quite natural that Duncan should sit behind me one morning at the weekly assembly and whisper to me without moving his lips. 'Are you going to Tony's on Saturday?'

'What's happening?'

'Party, Saturday night. His olds are going away.'

'Do they know he's partying?'

'What do *you* think?' He somehow made it sound like a smirk.

'Do you want me to come?'

'If you like.'

The following Saturday night Dunkie duly called at our door and escorted me to the car, which was driven by one of his mates and was already full of revellers. I don't know why I bothered going because I had already attended one or two similar functions, having told my parents that I was off to watch a video at a friend's house, and from the gossip in the common-room I knew that the many I had missed conformed exactly to the couple I had gone to.

Everyone crams into the house. The stereo is wound up so that the speakers are throbbing. People shout and whoop at each other, and the highlight of the evening is to see who vomits first. The young men achieve this slowly and steadily by consuming beer. Most of them get bloated and give up with a varying range of excuses, but one or two have reputations which depend on their performing at every social function they attend. My heart sank when I saw one notorious individual known as Spaghetti Guts lounging casually in the back seat of the vehicle conveying us to Tony's because wherever he went this specimen erupted as reliably and regularly as a geyser. I knew that if we were to transport him home after the night's revelries he would be pale and sweating, reeking horribly, and proclaiming his prowess in faint whispers.

The young ladies were more unpredictable. They tended to go for beverages such as rum and coke, gin and lemonade, rum and coke and lemonade, gin and lemonade and rum, and whatever else mine host could lay his hands on — what you might call pot-luck cocktails. The results could be spectacular and sudden.

Why did I do it? Because although I knew the evening would be dull, raucous, and probably nauseating, I lived in hope. There were times when I felt loneliness like an ache. I would pass a house at night and see a gathering of people through the curtains, raising glasses and talking and moving in a kind of joyous mime, with music faintly reaching the street, and I would suddenly long to be invited in. So when I *was* invited and my instincts and experience warned against accepting, I would wonder if this was to be one of those joyous nights and if I would always regret it if I stayed away.

So I went to Tony's and I regretted it and I left early, accepting the offer of a ride home from someone else who departed half-way through the evening. There was just one thing that made that night a little different. At one point in the middle of the crowd and noise I caught Dunkie's eye. He had appeared beside me once or twice during the evening, but mostly he had moved among his mates. Then at this moment I saw him standing alone leaning against the mantelpiece, and I caught his eye. He looked bored but his glance sharpened when he saw me. He smiled wryly and I think he was about to come over. But then someone shoved another can into his hand with some comment like, 'C'mon Dunkie, you've got to keep up mate!' and he accepted it, and the moment passed. He looked across at me almost defiantly as he peeled off the top and sucked in a mouthful, but I knew he was acting — and I think he realized I knew.

A few days later I asked Dunkie to take me to a movie, or rather I gave him an opportunity by dropping a heavy hint that I especially wanted to see this film. I did too, but I also suspected that if he were alone, good old Dunkie would become Duncan. I was almost right.

It was a week night and he was allowed his parents' car. He picked me up on time, we saw the movie, we both enjoyed it, we returned to the car. Then we drove to one of the local fast-food bars and bought hamburgers. It was my suggestion. 'Let's park down at the pits and eat these,' I said.

'All right,' said Duncan. I noticed a sort of tightness in his voice, but thought nothing of it at the time.

The pits should probably be spelled in capital letters. It was (and still is for all I know) an off-road parking area on the road leading down to the boat harbour. Overlooking the lake, just out of reach of the bright lights, it was the spot where the teenage good-old-boys gathered on weekend nights in their cars and planned where they were going to do wheelies that evening. While they were thinking deeply about this they downed a few cans, did a few practice runs up Tongariro Street, around the boat harbour and back to where they had started in order to think some more. In between these forays they communicated their feelings about cars at interminable length and eventually drove home to mother, squealing their tyres and gunning their engines in a kind of six-cylinder oratorio. If this account sounds somewhat cynical it's because I am reporting almost verbatim what was told to me by an acquaintance who made the mistake of agreeing to spend a Saturday evening with one of these cowboys, and was reduced to reading clothing labels to relieve the boredom.

On this night the pits were bare and vehicles of Japanese pedigree could safely graze without being hooted off by the Fords and Chevies. Dunkie pulled the car into a spot above the cliffs and switched off the engine. I noticed as I slowly munched that he was tearing into his bun and meat pattie impatiently and ferociously, with particles of coleslaw dropping away unnoticed. I sat back in the front seat, relaxing and watching the reflections from the main street lights slipping back and forth with the swell on the dark lake. I was still chewing when Dunkie finished, screwed up his paper bag and dropped it beside his seat. I was only half aware of what he was doing, but not for long. I had just closed my jaws over a delectable looking hunk of meat, with brown crispy edges, when Dunkie's arm swooped around behind me.

My mouth snapped shut like a spring trap and meat juice and mayonnaise dribbled down my chin. An instant later his mouth was pressed firmly against my ear, while his hand was up under my sweater making a bee-line for my bra. Well, not a bee-line exactly — more like a frantic crab out to make a kill. His free arm swung across me as he turned sideways, jarring my hand and shoving the helpless burger further into my mouth. At this precise moment I had a sudden vision of how utterly absurd this whole scene would look to someone peering through the windscreen. I burst into a hoot of laughter, sending a spray of mangled burger all over the dashboard, before collapsing into a violent coughing fit.

It was chaos of the most exquisite kind, all over

in a couple of seconds, something I could appreciate only afterwards when I reconstructed the order of events calmly and without prejudice. At the time, as soon as I had stopped laughing and coughing, I felt bewildered. Clearly Dunkie had made a pass at me, or rather a grab for me, but the speed of the attempted coup stunned me into temporary paralysis. He had retreated to his own side of the car and was slumped in the seat. Glancing at him I could see that he was staring out through the windscreen. Though I could not see the redness of his face, I could almost feel the heat of it.

Suddenly he hissed, 'Don't you ever tell anyone about this!'

My confusion evaporated and anger took over. 'Oh great, Dunkie! That's just great! You practically rape me and all you can worry about is someone hearing what a bloody mess you made of it!'

'Don't call me Dunkie!'

'Standing on our dignity are we? All right then, I'll call you Dunkin! Is that better Dunkin? Dunkin! Dunkin! Dunkin!'

I slammed myself back into my seat and bit my lip as I crashed my elbow against the door handle. So sudden was the silence that the flop of the waves on the beach below seemed to echo through the car. After a few moments of doom-laden quiet I tried a sideways glance without moving my head. He was trembling and I glimpsed beads of sweat under the black hair curled over his forehead. It was a delicate moment and I was briefly tempted to run through all the roles I could play and choose one: ridicule him as an oaf, play the outraged maiden and demand to be driven home forthwith, keep my mouth shut and let him make a bigger fool of himself . . .

Instead I put my hand on his arm and said the first

thing that came into my head: 'I thought you had Sally.'
I turned my head and smiled at him full-frontal and
waited.

To my relief he smiled back. 'Do you remember
that?' His arm stopped trembling. 'That was two years
ago.'

'Did Angie ever tell you what really happened?'

'Yeah, she told me. I gave her a belting.'

'You what?'

'Well, I thumped her one on the arm. God, that
was embarrassing.'

'For us all,' I said.

'And now I go and do this. I mean, I didn't know
how to — I haven't really known you ...'

'It's all right Duncan.'

'Don't call me Duncan, I hate it. Call me Dunkie.'

'But you just said ...'

'I know, but it depends on how you say it.'

I grinned. 'You don't want me to say it with feeling.'

'You've got the idea.'

By this time we had returned to such unconscious
ease that I was able to adjust the back of my sweater
without causing a flicker of reaction from either of us.
'I'll tell you what, Dunkie,' I said. 'Dad said he might
take the boat out at the weekend. Would you like to
come?'

'That'd be great,' he said eagerly. 'Will you be
fishing? I haven't been fishing for ages.'

'Sure to be,' I said. 'Now we'd better go home.'

'Just one thing. You wouldn't tell anyone ...'

'Our secret is safe with me.'

But I wasn't so sure about him. If I heard a whisper
about that evening there was going to be a sudden
unexplained cancellation of the weekend boating trip,
as far as he was concerned anyway. And if there was
a whisper to be heard, I could be certain that the senior

common-room grapevine would make sure a little spiky tendril would squirm its way to my ear. Oh faithless me! The following morning I was standing among a crowd at my locker completely out of sight. I heard a voice passing by.

'Did you make it last night, Dunkie?'

'Of course not. Didn't even try.'

His voice was as firm as a rock — no trace of a defensive whine. I felt bright all over.

The weekend matched my mood. We left early in the morning aiming to do a circuit round the Western Bay and Karangahape Cliffs, across to Horomatangi Reef for the evening fishing, then make the long haul back to the harbour as darkness fell. It was a classic Kemp expedition. Our launch was a graceful wooden-hulled vessel of a past age, built with kauri planks in the 1920s, about eight metres long, and still with its original engine. Flat out it could reach nine or ten knots, but my father rarely forced it to that speed. We cruised, with the bow wave curling to a comfortable height, the dinghy strutting behind on a leash of precisely the right length, and the whole launch moving across the slopes and contours of the swell in a way that made you remember always that you were floating on water. That might seem a strange thing to say, but if you have ever charged and bounced across a lake in a fibreglass launch, with a great black wart of an outboard engine snarling in your ear, you will know what I mean.

So our journeys were always leisurely. While my father sat on the edge of the hatch nudging the wheel occasionally with his foot, mother stretched out on a cockpit seat leaning against the cabin. She read or knitted or snoozed, waiting for the magic moment when the fishing started and she would be allowed to send her trusty gold cobra lure into the depths on a hundred metres of lead line and start slaughtering trout.

My mother's affection for birds and animals, and distaste for killing things, did not extend to the unfortunate rainbow trout. (She had never caught a brown trout and doubted their existence.) With a rod in her hand she was ruthless. To see this gentle woman, her hair greying and grandmotherly wrinkles beginning to crease the skin around her eyes, to see her reeling in a fish was enough to make you grateful that she had found a harmless outlet for her hunting instinct — unless you were a trout, of course.

She had no compunction, either, about bashing them on the head in the fish box after they had been netted. She didn't stun them, she sent them into instant oblivion with one fierce flick of the broken axe handle we used for the *coup de grâce*. On the trip back to the boat harbour she would kneel in the cockpit and gut the day's catch, setting aside the livers to make pate, and wrapping the remaining offal in newspaper for burial in the garden or compost heap. The next day she would preserve the fillets by bottling them in her venerable pressure cooker, adding a few more jars to the vast collection on the laundry shelves. That done, she would resume her normal routine and wait patiently for the next opportunity to be let loose over some bountiful reef.

My mother's lust for trout was one reason why expeditions such as the one we embarked on that Saturday were rare events. She preferred a quick dash out to Rangatira Point and a frenzied hour or two of screaming reels. But she always gave in to my father's wishes on these occasions because she knew that at certain times of the year the fishing round the Western Bay and Horomatangi Reef was well worth a long boat ride. On this particular day the signs were promising. As we rounded Rangatira Point and crossed the mouth of Mine Bay, we saw a huge patch of foam moving slowly across our bow — hundreds of trout feasting on clouds of smelt in a frenzied scatter across the surface of the lake.

'First time I've ever seen that,' my father said, 'though I've heard about it before.'

I noticed that my mother put down her book, idly reached for her fly tin and began picking over her smelt flies. But for me a journey like this over the depths of the lake always brought meandering into my head vague feelings of awe, and even dread. A return of the vision that had been echoed in Stanley Swinton's remark: 'You are looking at one of the most dangerous places on the face of the earth.'

After the long run to Waihaha, past the mouth of Kinloch Bay, my father always made for the cliffs and followed them around, moving as close as the wind and swell allowed. On a calm day the launch could slide past almost within touching distance of the rock walls reaching up from the depths. A fish hooked down there would be hauled to the light like a shivery blue phantom before it leapt in a splash of silver. I never thought of them as cliffs. I always imagined cliffs as belonging to the light and air, the margins of the land. These were walls of huge volcanic craters that happened to be filled with water curving from one horizon to the other, masking the awesome chasm that lay beneath, created when the land exploded.

This was one of my childhood nightmares, one of the dreams that always woke me. I am sure it must have begun as a memory of an early visit to Horomatangi Reef. Even as a seventeen-year-old, my skin tingled that day as we left the Karangahape Cliffs and made for the three-legged navigation beacon that marked the largest outcrop of the reef. My father or mother must have told me about the place when I was young enough to remember the message, but not old enough to recall the words. Since then I had made it my business to know the facts and I always found myself running over them with a kind of scientific detachment whenever I came near the place. It was, I suppose, my way of raising my defence shields, a means of keeping the nightmare vision at bay like the rituals that used to stop the witch emerging from the bathroom cupboard when you were first sent in alone to clean your teeth.

Duncan and I were leaning side by side against the mast as the reef came in sight. The sun was sinking, making the legs of the beacon glare white. So here comes the first fact. Fact Number One says that the white tripod carries more than a navigation beacon. It also provides a niche for a small, inconspicuous measuring device installed by some scientists for the purpose of recording the slightest movement of the rock outcrop on which the tripod rests. The reason for their interest will shortly become clear. For Fact Number Two we note the following information: the rock outcrop marks the only place where the reef breaks through the surface of the water, but in fact the whole reef covers an area of over two hundred hectares. In two other spots it comes to within two or three metres of the surface, one of them being a flat-topped pinnacle jutting from the depths like a pointing finger. You can find it by taking transit bearings from landmarks on the mountains that cradle the Taupo basin. When you pass over it you can see patches of weed blowing like hair on the pinnacle's crown.

So on to Fact Three which is best imparted by using a little imagery. You must think of this reef as a vast rock cauldron submerged in water, its rim reaching to the surface in these three places, one of them (as noted) breaking into daylight. The bottom of the cauldron marks the deepest point of the lake, and it lies a couple of hundred metres from the tripod. It also marks the vent from which the great Taupo eruption exploded about 1800 years ago, the youngest of the great cataclysms which created the lake.

For Fact Four you need to let your imagination loose and try to visualize what no one saw but for which the evidence remains, stretching like a shroud far across the North Island. When the vent over which we are now floating gaped open 1800 years ago and roared into life, it rammed into the sky a column of pumice dancing aloft to fifty kilometres in its fiercest burst — as far as the edge of space. Having cleared the throat of the vent, the column slowly collapsed into a fountain of red-hot viscous pumice which seethed over the edge of the cauldron and flowed overland at speeds reaching 600 kilometres an hour, before licking and lapping to a halt on hillsides and in valleys. When the turmoil died and the ground cooled and the lava hardened, the cauldron remained. It was drowned as the water filled the great chasm it had created and completed the construction of the watery panorama we know and love. Eat your heart out Krakatoa!

But the seeds of my childhood fears were planted deeper than facts. Facts can be handled. It is the 'what ifs' of this world that inspire nightmares and terror. My father had his favourite anecdote about the reef. He always told it to any guests on the boat whenever we circled around and over the place. I am sure I must have heard it first when I was very young, when it took root and thrived in my childhood dreams.

This day was no different. As the boat passed between the reef's high points he leaned forward and said, 'Does Duncan know about the geologist who was working here a few years ago?'

'I don't think so,' Dunkie said.

'Robbie's heard this before, but I've always thought it interesting. This chap was doing some research for a thesis. He was using an echo-sounder or something to study the depths of the old volcano vent, right below us. He had his supervisor with him, a professor I think. Anyway, he picked up a large patch of something near the bottom of the lake that was moving, and he said, "Must be a school of trout down there." But the professor said, "No, you just wait a couple of minutes and you'll see what it is." Then all of a sudden a huge patch of pumice shot up to the surface all around their launch and lay there bobbing up and down. Their launchman told me that. He said it looked like a white carpet.'

'Where did it come from?' Dunkie said.

'From the vent,' Dad replied. Then he lost interest and went back to steer the launch from the stern and do some fishing.

'It means that it's still alive,' I muttered, 'and that's why they've got a recorder on the tripod. They want to know if anything stirs.'

'It's still alive?'

'Yes, the volcano vent we are floating above is still alive — it's still active!' I said tensely.

Dunkie looked at me. 'Hey, you're trembling,' he whispered. 'Does it frighten you?'

'It used to terrify me,' I said. 'It still can.'

He tentatively put out one hand and slid it over mine, then held it firmly. 'One good turn deserves another,' he said. 'I promise not to tell anyone.'

He moved his arm behind me like a veteran and I quietly described to him my private vision of hell and forgot about fishing. I told him, too, about 'Kubla Khan' and the other reason why its words had burned into my mind when I first read it — something you will have noticed yourself if you know the poem and have read the last couple of pages with care and attention.

V
ELIZABETH AMELIA

During the happy months of that summer Duncan and I saw a lot of each other, yet I doubt if anyone noticed. It was a casual, undemanding friendship that was always there and did not mean the sacrifice of other interests or changes in our relationships with other people. For my part, other people hardly existed anyway, but he was still gregarious and outgoing. I noticed, though, that for Dunkie being with me was like a period of solitude which he sought out more and more frequently.

I was careful never to make him choose. If I phoned him to say that I was going to see a movie, or was planning a swim, I always made it clear that it would happen anyway, with or without him. He began to do the same. We were like birds, testing the limits of each other's territory, but beginning to enjoy the sensation of gliding gradually together towards an unknown stretch of the forest. He began coming with me occasionally to the Swintons, especially after school finished for the year and there were long days to fill if he didn't happen to be working.

By this time I had come to know the Swintons' estate very well and I often went there more than once a week. Mr Swinton commented on this after I had done it once or twice, perhaps suspecting that I was hoping eventually to lodge a supplementary pay demand. But I assured him that any extra labour was performed purely for love of the job. It was too. The truth was, I was quickly coming to enjoy Stanley's forest garden, especially when spring brought the trees to life and clustered whole groves of them with rich, scented flowers.

After rain the whole garden smelled wet. Insects hummed endlessly. All the trees seemed to make another lurch upwards and the upper canopies spread and twined like hands joining together. Standing among them I could imagine myself in the Amazon rain forests. One morning I said as much to Mr Swinton, and quickly discovered that he was a man who lived by the textbook with no time for flights of fancy.

He laughed. 'Your imagination has led you astray,' he said.

'I'm not saying this is a real jungle, but you can imagine what it would be like.'

'Can you? Can you imagine the gloom? Can you imagine the silence? Did you know that the rain forest is hushed and quiet during the day? No sun reaches the jungle floor. Did you know that?'

'I didn't say I knew what the jungle is really like,' I protested. 'I just meant that being here makes me think about it.'

'It reminds me of forests too,' he said. 'That's why I made it grow just the way I wanted it.' He ran his fingers through the soil at the base of a fern he had been planting, then cupping his hand he raised some to his nose. 'You can smell the goodness can't you? That's not like the real jungle either. The soil there is barren, completely barren. Isn't that strange?'

Absolutely bloody amazing, I thought to myself. I had finished mowing for the morning and began to push the mower back up to the garage. Thinking I would make my exit with a safe, frivolous remark I said, 'There aren't any nasties in your jungle either.' I should have known better.

'Nasties?'

'Nothing dangerous you need to watch out for. Snakes, jaguars and nasty insects. Or don't you find those in the real jungle either?'

'What makes you think there is nothing dangerous in my jungle?'

He was challenging me, looking me in the eye. 'Perhaps you can't see it. Perhaps it will get you when you least expect it.'

When he smiled his golden fang gleamed from the brown, scarred face, and his attempt at humour was forced. It had occurred to me that Mr Swinton was possibly loopy, but not alarmingly so — more your average harmless eccentric with a vivid imagination. In fact I had once realized with a shudder that I might grow into something resembling him if I didn't watch myself. But I had never seen him as a potential menace, nor did I now. All the same, he seemed to be obsessed with something, teasing me by letting me see it was there. So let that be a lesson to you, I thought, as I wheeled the mower into the garage — don't make harmless remarks to Stanley about rain forests.

'Coffee this morning, dear?'

With her usual uncanny timing, Elizabeth Amelia appeared at the front door of the garage like a genie minus her puff of smoke.

'Not today thank you Mrs Swinton. I have to get home.'

Next time then — and please call me Elizabeth, dear.'

Then she vanished. She was one of those people who have to be watched very carefully if you wish to see them move from one place to another. She was like a friendly, bespectacled wraith, an impression heightened when she was clad in one of her ponchos, the garment she was wearing when I first made her acquaintance. After I had been visiting the house for several weeks, and the cold September southerlies had died away, the heavy woollen ponchos gave way to elaborately embroidered capes and cloaks which she always wore outdoors, and frequently inside as well. She always seemed prepared to swish into the air, or transform a pumpkin into a coach.

At first I had marked her down as pure vegetable herself, because on my early visits she was forever offering me pikelets. I hate the damn things, probably because they are one of my mother's disaster areas. She can produce featherweight pavlovas on demand, but her pikelets used to resemble circles of brown or black leather. I think she thought them too humble to be worth bothering about. She no longer attempts them.

Mrs Swinton was not deterred by my constant refusals and soon came up with scones, which I accepted gratefully, though by this time I was convinced I was visiting the lair of a thoroughbred New Zealand home-maker who ironed her husband's underpants. The ponchos puzzled me though, especially when I checked the clothes-line for cardigans and twin sets with a complete lack of success. I could have been prejudiced by the homely Victorian overtones of her second name — Amelia. I remember I actually checked in the electoral roll to see what it was. Stanley didn't have a second name. I was very nosy in those days.

One Saturday morning she invited me inside instead of bringing the provisions down to the garden to eat from the bird-table. After that, coffee in the front room became a habit, unless I had other things to do. At first we chatted about nothing in particular — the weather, how I was doing at school, and so on. But after the third or fourth occasion she began to converse with me, and the subject of Stanley would surface in our little talks, quite naturally with no prompting from me. It was as though she wanted to make me better acquainted with him, having decided that I seemed to be a fixture.

One Saturday morning I followed her inside for

cheese scones and coffee and asked if I should call Mr Swinton.

'Oh no,' she replied, 'you must have noticed that he never joins us for morning coffee.'

Of course I had, and I was wondering why but could hardly ask outright.

'He finds social small talk and chit-chat not to his liking,' she continued, 'especially with strangers, and that means with anyone except me.' She peered at me over her spectacles as she nestled herself in a pile of cushions on the window seat. 'He is a very solitary man — I suppose we are both solitary people — but you mustn't think Stanley regards you as an outsider. In fact I think he is rather taken with you.'

That was interesting information. Taken with me in what respect?

'Do you have any brothers or sisters, Robbie?'

'No,' I said, 'I'm an only child.'

'Do you wish you had?'

'Sometimes. I suppose it would be nice to have someone else young around the place.'

'Of course it would, and I think Stanley thinks the same way about you. It's nice to have someone your age coming to see us every week, and of course he is very pleased with the way you work.'

'Is he?' I mumbled, caught with a mouthful of scone. 'He's never told me that.'

'Well, he wouldn't,' said Mrs Swinton. 'He's not a demonstrative man. He keeps himself to himself.'

It occurred to me that even a raving introvert shouldn't find it that difficult to tell someone she's doing a good job. But I let it pass because the conversation was veering in a direction to my liking.

'Your own children must have left home long ago,' I said innocently.

'We had a daughter,' said Mrs Swinton. 'She

departed several years ago.'

She let that remark sink in, gazing at me reflectively as I scrambled for another scone and snatched a mouthful. What did she mean by 'departed?'

'She wasn't much older than you at the time. Stanley felt her loss very deeply. I did too, naturally, but it hit him particularly hard and changed him in many ways.'

'What was her name?' I asked.

'Cecilia.'

Cecilia Swinton. What a mouthful! Samuel Taylor would have had fun with that.

'We called her Celie,' said Mrs Swinton. 'It wasn't a happy choice of name when you have to say it quickly.'

I began to wonder who was in charge of this conversation. 'I'm called Robbie, but I'm really Robyn,' I said weakly.

'Through choice, I imagine, rather than necessity,' said Mrs Swinton.

I nodded agreement and for some reason felt furious with myself. She was sitting there on the window-seat, her feet tucked under her, and she was getting all the good lines. There was more to Elizabeth Amelia than her tiny grandmotherly frame suggested. There was a touch of steel in her cropped grey hair and the twinkle in her eye betrayed a knowingness that I was beginning to find unsettling.

'Perhaps you would like to see a photograph of our daughter.' Without waiting for a reply she walked to the sideboard and rummaged amongst a pile of old folders and papers in the bottom drawer. 'It's so dusty in here,' she said, drawing out a framed photograph and handing it to me. 'There she is — our daughter.' She placed it on my lap, then went over to her spinning-wheel that was set up as a permanent fixture in one corner of the room. 'Take your time with your coffee. I'll just get on with this fleece. I can talk as I go.'

What she meant was, 'Have a good hard look at the photograph, my dear, while I watch your reactions.' She would have seen, as I'm sure she expected, a look of utter astonishment on my face. Looking up at me was a girl who could have been taken for my twin at a glance. She had the same blonde hair cut to shoulder length, the eyebrows were heavy like mine, and a band of freckles spread from one cheek to the other across a short, tilted nose. Our expressions were different, I think, but at a casual look the resemblance was startling. For a while I just stared, listening to the spinning wheel whirring. I knew she was waiting, probably watching me intently. It was a relief to hear her speak first.

'Quite astonishing isn't it? When you came to the door that day I was almost afraid to call Stanley. I thought the sight of you might scare him to death. But really, it's a superficial resemblance. Celie always had a solemn set to her mouth, while you always look as though you're amused at something.'

'It's certainly a coincidence,' I said. I was completely out of snappy replies.

'On that first day when you came to inquire about the job, I was listening while Stanley talked to you.'

She wanted me to ask the reason.

'I didn't know that,' I said.

'Well, you wouldn't would you? I pretended to walk to another room, but I hid around the corner in the hallway. I didn't know how Stanley would react to you. He could have done two things. He could have sent you away, or he could have mastered the shock he must have felt when he first saw you and come to terms with you.'

'By giving me the job?'

'By being willing to have a constant reminder of

his daughter coming here every week — and more often these days, it seems.'

'What did you expect him to do?'

'I thought he would send you away at once. I was pleasantly surprised when he didn't. I think it was something you said that tipped the balance.'

'What was that?'

'You said something about admiring his gold filling.'

'I remember,' I said. 'Actually I only said that because — well, because — '

'Because you were startled by his scarred skin?'

'Yes. I mean, I didn't think it was horrible or anything, it was just so unexpected.'

'That's understandable, and there's no denying that Stanley has a most unusual face. But your mention of the golden tooth was a lucky move. From the time Cecilia was very young she was fascinated by that gold filling. Even before she could talk she would sit on his knee and force his lips open so she could rub her finger against it. Then when she was a little older she would polish it with a handkerchief. She loved its gleam.'

By now I needed no further convincing that the young Cecilia was definitely turned on by her old man's gold filling.

'It was just a coincidence that I mentioned it,' I said.

'Naturally,' said Mrs Swinton. She had brought the spinning-wheel to rest and was replacing the spool. 'But to some people coincidences are not without significance, and I'm sure that Stanley saw Cecilia in you at that moment. As you can see from the photograph, there's an uncanny resemblance.' She came over to me and removed the picture from my lap.

'Why don't you have it hanging?' I asked.

'It was once on the wall with the others.' She pointed to the panelled wall above the bookcase which

46

was covered with an array of photographs and prints. 'A few years ago Stanley replaced it and put it away in the drawer. I think it was a reminder of Cecilia that he didn't wish to look at day in and day out. It used to hang there.' She walked to the wall and indicated a reproduction of a water-colour showing the southern end of Lake Taupo. 'Do you know this? It was painted by Barraud in 1874. Stanley always chuckles at the animals grazing in the foreground — taming the wild landscape, he says.'

I had followed her to the painting. 'It certainly looks calm and peaceful.'

'Doesn't it? It's been a scene that always amuses Stanley for some reason. He stands in front of it sometimes with a grim smirk on his face as though to say, "We'll do something about you one of these days." Most odd, wouldn't you agree? Well, I must get on, my dear, and I suppose you have things to do.'

I was shooed out the door as though a consultation was over. I was tempted to stand my ground and ask why the photograph of the late departed Cecilia was as clean as a polished jewel if it had lain neglected so long in a dusty drawer, but I thought better of it.

When Duncan first came up to the Swintons' property I could see so many questions in his eyes that I had to warn him off. I knew enough now about Stanley to suspect that anyone who pried too openly into his affairs would be shown the gate. Dunkie's introduction to the Swintons came one Saturday morning. I had finished the lawns and was about to go when I heard a commotion in one of the cedar trees on the back boundary. On investigating I discovered Mr Swinton clinging to the trunk about half-way up trying to saw a branch that jutted over the neighbour's fence. He was hanging on with his right hand and trying to move the saw with his left, and not making much impression.

He paused for breath and saw me standing below. 'I'm trying to trim this branch,' he gasped. 'Neighbour's been complaining.'

'Would you like some help?'

'I'm not sure what you could do. The problem is, I can't get at it with my right hand.'

'You need someone who's left-handed,' I said.

'Very true. Are you left-handed?'

'No, but I know someone who is.'

'So do I, but I doubt if he'd want to clamber up a tree to trim a branch.'

'The friend I'm thinking of wouldn't mind.'

I could see him thinking this over. Stanley was very proud of his little forest and it irked him when he had to allow other hands to touch anything in it. Early in my career at the Swintons I had offered to prune back some camelias that were overhanging part of the lawn, and he had looked at me as though I were suggesting arboreal rape. Of course, it was all right if he did it, when it doubtless became severance of limbs between consenting species.

Nevertheless, on this occasion he was agreeable to my summoning my friend who, naturally, turned out to be Dunkie. Dunkie was actually more ambidextrous than left-handed, but he could attempt most things with his left hand, as I had discovered during that memorable evening in the front seat of his car. He arrived about ten minutes after my phone call and I hastily hushed him as I led him down to the rear of the section. He was as entranced by Stanley's jungle as I had been when I first saw it. He was up the tree like an ape, his lanky body embracing the trunk as though he had been born to a life in the foliage. Tree climbing was a talent I never knew Dunkie possessed.

I managed to clamber up the fence and loop a rope

around the offending branch. While Stanley and I hauled it back towards home territory with all our combined weight behind it, Dunkie sawed. Eventually it snapped off and cascaded in a whoosh of leaves and insects at our feet. Duncan descended in a few Tarzanesque pirouettes and we all three stood around the remains looking smug.

'I'm very grateful to you — Duncan, did you say?'

That's right, Duncan McDonald. My friends call me Dunkie.'

'Do they really? Well, you have certainly been of great assistance.' Stanley looked at us both like a monarch dismissing his faithful retainers.

I knew Dunkie was dying to stay around longer to see more of the place. 'Would you like us to get rid of the branch, Mr Swinton?'

'There's really no need. I can manage now.'

'No trouble at all,' Dunkie said. 'I'm sure you've got other things to do, and Robbie and I would be glad to help.'

Don't start overacting, sunshine, I thought, or he'll turn us down just to spite us. But his eyes were as close as they ever came to twinkling. He knew I was eager for a chance to give Dunkie a conducted tour of the property. 'All right,' he said. 'As a matter of fact I do want to get on turning the compost. Just drag the branch up to the trailer at the back of the garage.' Then he strode off through the trees, his white hair looking ghost-like as he moved in and out of the shadows.

I turned to Duncan. 'Now you've met Stanley Swinton.'

'And this is his garden! I never believed it when you told me. A tiny forest in suburbia. Let's take our time dragging this away so I can look around.'

We manoeuvred the branch out of the tall trees at the back of the section and on to the lawned alley-ways among the smaller trees and shrubs. Pausing for breath, Duncan said, 'It's really very cunning, you know. He's designed it like a maze so that at every turn you think you're in the open, but you're not. It seems as though it goes forever. Did you get lost when you started here?'

'Only if I pretended to be lost. The trouble is, the ground rises so you always know your way out.'

We hauled the amputated limb up to the trailer, then Duncan insisted on staying and walking further around the garden. He was curious about the place and its owner. He wanted to know everything that I knew.

'Where does he come from? Why did he plant all this?'

'How would I know?'

'You must know something about him.'

'He told me he's been to South America. It must have been when he was quite young. That's where he picked up smallpox — you can see the scars on his face.'

'Right, I noticed those. I've a couple of miniature versions on my back from where I had chickenpox. Whereabouts in South America?'

'I've no idea, though he's talked once or twice about the jungle.'

'The Amazon rain forest,' said Dunkie. 'I'll bet he's wandered around the Amazon, or in the Mato Grosso. Full of rain forests, they are. Colonel Fawcett disappeared in the Mato Grosso. Did you know that?'

'I can't say I did. Who's Colonel Fawcett?'

'I read about him in a book my Dad got for a Sunday school prize when he was a kid. Happened years ago when the Mato Grosso was a real wilderness. He disappeared in the jungle and was never seen or heard of again.'

'What did he go in there for?'

'I can't remember. I think he was looking for a lost city or something.'

'Well, there isn't a lost city in this lot,' I said, 'only that.' I pointed to Stanley's aquarium building hiding against the fence.

'I would have walked right past it,' said Duncan. 'What is it?'

'Stanley's aquarium. He breeds fish in there.'

'What kind of fish?'

'I've no idea. They must be tropical fish, I suppose, because he heats the building from the steam bore. But I've never been in there.'

'Why not?'

'Because he won't let me, possibly because the lawn ends before you reach the door, and I'm employed to mow the lawns!'

'Sarcastic, aren't we? Why aren't there any windows in the place?'

'Dunkie, I don't know!'

'All right, all right. But aren't you curious?'

We had arrived at the door of the small building and Dunkie pressed his ear against it like a nosy butler in one of those faded tales about foul doings in a decrepit English manor hall. 'They must be pretty big fish.'

'Why?'

'I can hear water swirling around. Come and listen.'

'Dunkie, would you come away? I know what's going to happen. This is going to be a cliché come to life. I know it! Stanley's going to appear from behind a tree or something.'

I was close. At that precise moment Stanley opened the door and said, 'And here I am, right on cue! I was adjusting one of the air inlets.'

Dunkie put his mouth into neutral and waited.

'The water swirling,' said Mr Swinton.

'Oh,' said Dunkie, 'that would explain it, all right. Air being forced into water.'

I was tempted to let him talk his own way out of the situation, but took pity on him. 'I've finished Mr Swinton. We'd better be off. See you next week.'

We crept away like a couple of prize insects, our dignity shredded.

'Oh, Duncan!'

When we looked back, Stanley was still leaning against the door, grinning. 'Please don't feel I'm ordering you off the property. I don't mind if you pop up from time to time when Robyn is working here. I really am grateful for the help you gave me.' Then he disappeared inside.

'What's his wife like?' Duncan muttered.

'She's a real sweetie too,' I said. 'You know, I think he likes you. That's only the second time I've ever seen him grinning.'

VI
AQUARIUM

Over the summer months Dunkie often turned up when I was working at the Swintons. He always claimed to be on his way to somewhere else, or coming to see if I wanted to join him on some enterprise or excursion, but I knew that he found the Swintons' place interesting. Like me, he enjoyed lounging among the trees on a hot summer's morning, or standing in the silent gloom of the big grove of tall trees at the back. Down there the ground was almost devoid of undergrowth or vegetation of any kind. The sun was shut out by the high foliage and only a few delicate ferns grew in the damp humus.

On the sunnier mounds, Mr Swinton cultivated herbs along the borders and carefully mulched them with compost which he tended with loving care. He said the herbs added fragrance to the garden. I don't recall him ever picking any for use in the kitchen. He spent hours at his compost bins, turning the coarser material with a garden fork, and sifting the rest with his hands, crumbling the lumps with his fingers and grunting with delight when he came across clumps of worms.

He always greeted Duncan's arrival with a different sort of grunt, though he was never unpleasant. I think he accepted him as part of the scenery, something that passed through occasionally like the tui who visited the flax bush as part of its daily round. But from time to time he questioned me about Dunkie, usually making idle enquiries about where he lived, how long I had known him, what he did at school and that kind of thing.

On one particular afternoon I discovered that he

53

paid much more attention to Duncan and me than I had ever imagined. Dunkie had appeared briefly to arrange a trip to the beach after I had finished and had left almost at once. Mr Swinton had seen him arrive but had gone back up to the house and couldn't have seen him go. Meanwhile, I had disappeared down to the back of the garden to rake some dead leaves from one of the paths.

I was feeling hot and sweaty when I finished and walked into the grove of big trees to rest for a few minutes and let the shadows cool me. I was leaning against a tree watching a fantail high above me prancing and shying through the branches when I heard scuffling footsteps. Looking around I saw Stanley. He was trying to give the impression of a man taking a relaxed stroll, but he was turning and wheeling in all directions. His eyes were swivelling like oiled bearings and his mouth was pressed into a hard line. I thought he must have lost his gold filling, though he didn't seem to be carrying out a systematic search.

'Lost something?' I said.

He hadn't realized I was so near. He couldn't see into the gloom. He stopped with a startled, 'Oh, there you are!' and his lips spread into a forced smile, revealing the familiar gleam safely at home. As I walked into the sunlight he said, 'Duncan has gone, has he?' He sent a few shifty glances over my shoulder into the shadows.

'He went about ten minutes ago.'

'I didn't notice. I came down to see if you had finished. Anything need doing in here?' He walked right into the grove of trees and strode around slapping tree trunks like a stud-master patting the rumps of his favourite stallions. By this time I was darned sure what was on his suspicious little mind. Robbie plus Dunkie disappearing down the back among the tall trees equalled Robbie and Dunkie having a frolic among the ferns. The colt appeared to have gone but he wanted to make sure.

He didn't look at me when he emerged but rambled on about having to clear up more overhanging branches before long. He walked beside me up the path using a gait which I had come to recognize as a sign that he wanted to say something important. He would lengthen his stride, thumping his heels into the ground like a goose-stepping soldier, shove his hands deep into his pockets and gaze into the middle distance, never meeting your eye. He had fallen into this weird ritual once before when he wanted to tell me to stop weeding one of the herb gardens which was full of rare plants. It was his way of showing that he felt awkward.

'I had a daughter once,' he said.

'I know. Mrs Swinton mentioned her to me.'

'Did she? She's talked to you about Cecilia, has she?'

'Not very much,' I replied hastily. 'I asked her one day if you had any children and she said that you once had a daughter.'

'She's gone now. You remind me of her in many ways,' he said after a moment.

I wasn't sure what he was building up to and thought it best to keep quiet and not reveal any details of my conversation with Elizabeth Amelia concerning the departed Cecilia. I waited.

'I cared for her deeply.'

Did you love her? I wondered.

'Young people need protecting,' he said.

We had reached the front of the house and were standing and looking out over the lake. He had adopted one of his Easter Island statue poses, where he lowered his chin into his neck and let his eyes suggest that he was pondering the mysteries of the universe.

'Young people are threatened by so many dangers

they are only half aware of,' he continued. 'Do you agree?'

'Absolutely,' I said. Surely he didn't imagine that good old Dunkie was a dangerous phenomenon!

'Cecilia had a friend about her own age. They got on well together. He was a likeable lad.'

Now I was interested. What had Celie been up to at about my age?

'What happened?' I asked.

'It came to an end,' he said. He broke out of his reverie and strolled further towards the front fence so that he was looking at his prize-winning view. 'There are a lot of launches out on the lake today.'

'The trout are smelting,' I said. 'It's good for harling at the moment. My parents were out a couple of days ago and Mum caught a limit at Mine Bay.'

'Do you fish yourself?'

'Not as much as she does. My Mum's a killer when the trout are on.'

'Trout and smelt,' Stanley said. 'Where would Taupo be without trout and smelt?'

I smiled one of those inane expressions that mean what anyone pleases.

'That wasn't an idle question,' he said sharply.

Sorry Mr Swinton, sir, my mistake!

'Have you ever thought what this lake would be like with no smelt and no trout?'

'I suppose it would be water and not much else,' I said.

'That's right,' he replied, 'just water. No fishing. No fishing launches. It would be a catastrophe for this town, wouldn't it?'

'I suppose so. I guess people would just have to go water-skiing.'

He wouldn't leave the subject alone. 'The smelt and the trout were introduced to the lake, you know. They are not indigenous.'

'I know.'

'Someone even released goldfish into the lake many years ago. Were you aware of *that*?'

'No, I must say I didn't know about that one.'

'You'd be surprised what exists under all that water,' he said. Then he wandered inside and I, with some relief, made my escape. I had endured Stanley's contemplative rambles more than once and I found them tiring. It was like following a piece of string that began nowhere and ended up in the same place.

Which goes to show that I should have been more alert on that particular day and knitted a few loose threads together. When I thought about it carefully I realized that almost everything that happened later had been portended. But I did not blame myself. What did happen was so outlandish that you would have had to be eccentric yourself to foretell it. Nevertheless, both Dunkie and I had been in Mr Swinton's company enough to know that he had possibilities in the realms of the bizarre. Dunkie phrased it more bluntly: 'I reckon he could be round the twist.'

Both of us began to pay particular attention to Mr Swinton. In Duncan's case this meant an almost obsessive concentration on the aquarium building. It fascinated him, mainly because we were not allowed to see inside. He wasn't with me every week, of course. For most of the time I spent my hour or so at the Swintons alone, mowing the avenues and sometimes raking dead leaves or trimming edges. Even when Duncan showed up I was usually left to my own devices. He would sit, or walk about in an apparently aimless fashion, but always where he could peer through branches or under a tree at the door of the aquarium.

Over the summer months his vigilance was

rewarded. He collected a couple of snippets of information. First of all he noticed that the thermal bore seemed to be falling into disuse.

'How do you know?' I asked.

'There's hardly any steam coming out of it these days. He's turned it down.'

'The weather's getting warmer. There's no need for it.'

'But if he's been using it to raise the temperature of the water, it wouldn't matter what the weather was like. I mean, sunshine wouldn't compensate for the heat loss, would it? Anyway, have you noticed that he's keeping the skylight wide open? I reckon he's cooling the place down.'

'What if he is?'

'I don't know,' Duncan said. 'I'd just like to find out what he's doing.'

Then he noticed something that I wouldn't have thought twice about. Stanley usually fed his fish in the late afternoon or early evening. I never had the chance to observe this ritual when I first started working there, but after daylight saving started I sometimes delayed going up there until after tea so that I could avoid the heat of the day. On several occasions I saw Stanley make his way to the aquarium carrying a plastic ice-cream container, sometimes two of them, which presumably held the evening fodder for his precious fish.

As far as I was concerned, that was it. Dunkie was the one who spotted the oddity. 'Have you ever noticed the way that cat always follows Stanley down from the house when he's feeding the fish?'

'I can't say I have. Which cat are you talking about?' I replied.

'That mean looking tabby thing.'

'I think it belongs next door. I've seen it disappear through the fence a few times.'

'So it doesn't belong to the Swintons?'

'No, they don't own anything on four legs.'

'That means that the cat knows to come over here at about the time Stanley sets out to fill the fishes' feeding trough.'

'Yes Dunkie,' I said with great force and clarity, 'I suppose it does! What does all this mean Dunkie?'

'Why would a cat follow him?'

'I don't know!'

'There's no need to snap.'

'I'm not snapping. I'm expressing a profound sense of exasperation! Perhaps the bloody cat is hoping to slip in undetected and put a few goldfish out of their misery. Who knows? Or maybe the soft animal likes having an evening stroll with his friendly neighbour.'

Poor Dunkie. I should have paid more attention to him. But on his next visit, about three weeks later, Dunkie struck lucky. As he arrived he passed Mr Swinton driving down the road away from the house. He scuttled down the back, greeted me briefly through the roar of the mower engine, then darted quickly towards the aquarium. I was cutting a swathe around one of Stanley's prize rhododendron groves and rounded the corner in time to see Dunkie crouched behind a shrub.

He turned and saw me. I was about to switch off the engine when he flapped his hand back and forth and shook his head vigorously. Then he waved me over. I got the message: Leave the engine running and proceed over here forthwith. I obeyed. I was in time to see Mrs Swinton unlock the door of the aquarium. In Stanley's absence Elizabeth Amelia did feeding duty. I had the impression that she found the experience distasteful. She was having difficulty unlocking the door and had placed the plastic container at her feet. When the door swung open at last she picked up the container with thumb and forefinger on either side of the rim, as though its contents offended her. She was inside for about a minute. When she emerged she slammed the door shut, banged the container upside down against the door-frame and hurried back up towards the house.

As soon as she was out of sight, Dunkie sped over to the door like a ferret after a chicken and pressed his ear to the woodwork. I hadn't moved. Suddenly his face lit up and he turned back to me.

'Come here, quickly! Hurry!'

'All right, all right!'

'Listen! Put your ear to the door!'

There was no need to do that. I could hear it — a persistent and urgent thrashing of water as though it was being beaten by a flail.

Dunkie stood up. 'What on earth can he be keeping in there? It sounds like a shark going berserk.'

'It's probably his filtration system having a fit,' I said, 'disturbing the water to mix in the oxygen, or something like that.'

'Would it make that much noise?'

'Who knows? But it's certainly more likely than a shark.' I moved away from the door, then stopped. I felt something soft under my sneaker that slid against the sole. I snatched my foot away.

'What is it?'

'I've trodden on something. If it's a dog turd again I'll —.'

Stuck to the sole of my sneaker was a small piece of meat. I picked it off delicately and held it up for inspection.

'She banged the container when she came out,' said Dunkie.

'Now we know why the cat stuck close to Stanley,' I muttered, 'except today he forgot, which was tough luck for him.'

'Robbie,' said Duncan, 'are you sure it's fish that Stanley is rearing in there? I mean, who feeds fish on raw meat? Especially meat with bits of bone in it.' He pointed to a white sliver poking out of the morsel of mutton, or whatever it was.

'Maybe he's got something chained up in there,' I suggested.

'Why the water?'

'A big drinking trough?'

'Why doesn't whatever it is make a noise?'

'Perhaps he's on to a new breed of cat that doesn't miaow,' I said.

'I think there are cats around like that already. Mind you, it would explain the moggie from next door being so interested in the place. You know, somehow we really must get a look inside there. Got to go — I'm haymaking tomorrow. See you!'

'Make lots of money!' I called.

'I will. Have fun back at school.'

The following morning I would be starting my last year of school, as a seventh former. Dunkie, due to depart for university in March, was earning money working for a local haymaking contractor. 'Have fun back at school,' he said. He was up near the top of the path when he called out. He turned back, sort of running sideways, with a broad grin on his face. That was all I took in. I was only glancing in his direction, but I rebuilt him in my mind again and again as he was at that moment, because that was the last time I ever saw Dunkie. Not much more than twelve hours later he was dead.

VII
ACCIDENT

While I was at my first day of school for my last year, he was out in some farmer's paddock heaving haybales. He had the use of the family car for the day to drive out there. He had a mate with him. Normally they would have travelled to the farm in the contractor's truck, but on this day his employer had left earlier than usual and could not give them a lift.

They worked late until sundown, hurrying to get the last bales in because rain was forecast for the following day. By the time they had cleaned up, the sun had gone and they set out for home in the dusk. Everyone else in the gang stayed to drink a can or two of beer to wash the dust and seeds from their mouths and throats, but Dunkie and his friend decided not to remain. They had nothing to drink except water.

Dunkie was not speeding. The road was unsealed and he took care on the metalled surface. They were in no hurry. The Taupo lights burst into view as they came over the brow of a hill, and they drove down the gentle slope on the other side. They could see Mount Tauhara silhouetted black against the evening sky. It was a clear night. At the bottom of the hill the road took a sharp left turn before sweeping down to the sealed highway. The bend usually had a large white arrow warning motorists of the sudden change of direction. It was painted on a wooden barrier erected on the far verge of the bend. Beyond it there was nothing. The shoulder of the road fell away in a bank about a metre high. Without the barrier there was nothing to show that the road veered suddenly. On that night the barrier was not there.

Dunkie had seen the danger and braked, but he

was too late. The car skidded and shuddered into a broadside across the loose metal. It flipped over the bank and fell to solid ground on its roof, with its wheels spinning in the air. Dunkie's friend was shaken and bruised in a few places but was able to crawl out. Dunkie was killed. His head struck the door pillar. Dunkie's friend told me about it. The doctor told the post-mortem later that Dunkie had been very unlucky to die. Normally one would expect someone properly belted into his seat to have a good chance of surviving such an accident.

The warning barrier was not far away, lying in a paddock where the vandals who had broken it up had thrown it. They had destroyed it three days before and tried to light a fire with it. There had been a delay in getting a replacement in position because the proper timber had not been available at the works depot. What bad luck!

What bad luck that someone who had not been drinking or speeding or doing wheelies should flip his car over a bank and hit his head in just the wrong place and be killed instantly, while I was having fun on my first day back at school for my last year, and he was making lots of money, because he was going off to university in March.

It was my first death. One or two aunts and uncles I hardly knew had passed away, but this was my first death. I went to school the following morning. There was an assembly and I sat in the back row on the left-hand side in my civilian clothes. Rows of uniforms spread the length of the hall. Teachers stood around the edges against the walls. We all looked up at the stage, hollowed out like a curtained cave at the far end. Someone from up there talked about Duncan McDonald and the accident that had killed him. He told us how we were all at risk at our age and how no one could really protect us from the dangers we had to learn about through experience. Then someone read some notices, and I asked myself why we couldn't keep on talking about it, but I was surrounded by whispering mouths and the smell of school-bags and the jangling bells ringing all day, and I couldn't think about anything anyway.

My mother accompanied me to the funeral. I sat about half-way back and watched and listened. I saw people filing in. Some of them knelt and bowed their heads, then sat back and murmured. I stared at the stained glass window high up at the front, then at the dark, stained timber walls. The organist shuffled sheets of music and began playing softly. Duncan's family filed in and sat in the front pews that had been reserved for them. They were led in by the minister who was dressed in a white surplice, and he was murmuring too. Then he stepped to the front and began speaking in clear tones. I tried to concentrate on his face, but I could not stop my gaze slipping past him and across the dull glimmer of the brass handles, and finally I gave in and looked at the coffin.

I knew that I shouldn't, that I was surrendering my shield, but I could not resist any longer and I stared at the dark polished wood trying to stop myself looking inside. Shutting my eyes as we sang a hymn, I chanted to myself over and over again, 'close your eyes with holy dread, for he on honey-dew hath fed,' in time to the music, and I felt my mother's hand on my arm dragging me down when the hymn was over. But no matter how fiercely I pushed it away, Dunkie's face floated into my eyes, calm and peaceful and pale, except for a purple bruise at the side of his forehead. He would not go away. He looked at me and started saying, 'Have fun back at school, have fun back at school,' and suddenly I felt all the knots holding me together loosening at once. With a kind of choking noise I let go with what must have been the biggest flood of tears ever seen in that church, my whole body rigid and shaking so that my mother's protective arm seemed to be bumping up and down against my shoulders.

I was so unprepared. I had no strategy, no defence. I did not know what to expect. I was alone. I had to let it all slam into me and wait until it was over. I don't recall much of the funeral service after that. I remember walking out of the church and having consciously to think about placing my feet one after the other. The bright afternoon sun after the dark building bleached everything white and people's faces swayed back and forth with their mouths moving.

When the world came back into focus I found myself in the front seat of the car and my mother saying, 'Robbie! Are you all right? Robbie?'

'Yes, I'm all right.'

'I said that we wouldn't go back to the house. I think we'd better get you home.'

'Back to the house?'

'To the McDonald's house.'

'Why do we have to go there?'

'We don't. The mourners have been invited back to the house, but we don't have to go.'

'Where are they taking — where is he going?'

'The internment is for close family only. Anyway, I doubt if you could have stood up to it. We'll go home.'

I said suddenly, 'I want to go to the house.'

My mother looked at me sharply. 'Robbie, are you sure? You look in a state of utter shock to me.'

'I want to go. I want to see.'

'It'll just be people standing around eating a few biscuits and having a cup of tea.'

'I'm feeling all right now. I'd like to go. I'd like a cup of tea.'

'Very well, if you say so. It would be nice to put in an appearance. It would mean so much to Mrs McDonald.'

The house was full of people, some of whom I knew, but mostly they were strangers to me — relatives and family friends from other places. By the time we arrived they were standing in bunches conversing with tight little mouths, sipping tea or beer or the beverage of their choice, and nibbling at sausage rolls and sandwiches. I cannot explain my reaction, or even why I wanted to go there. Perhaps I was looking for someone to despise. I have been to other funerals since and have come to appreciate the need for people to escape from the ceremonies of death into the ordinary comforts of sausage rolls, scones, and cups of tea as soon as possible.

As the uncle said, 'Life must go on.'

Or the aunt, 'It's a blessing he went so quickly.'

'He couldn't have felt a thing,' said another.

'Marion is bearing up well, isn't she?'

Marion was Dunkie's mother and she had just returned, red-eyed and pale, with the family group.

I was too naïve to realize that they dared not speak their real thoughts. Even worse, in my arrogance I fondly imagined that I alone suffered. When I grew older I learned that we all have our personal jungles that grow from private myths and fears. We imagine them as dark and impenetrable and we cringe from them. But then? Then I was affronted at what I saw and heard and I felt myself shrivelling back into a hard knot, back to square one where I could puzzle things out.

Worst of all, I found myself thinking of my parents as strangers, especially my father. At the time I thought he was cold and unsympathetic. He said very little to me when Dunkie died, though I should have noticed that he took care to be around me a great deal during those first few days. The problem was me. I now knew what he must have felt at the death of my brother, and the knowledge embarrassed me. All those years, and I had never known what the photograph of a two-year-old boy really meant to him. I was afraid to imagine what he might have thought when he looked at me. If he had felt as I was feeling now, what would he have seen? I was too frightened to let the picture swell and mature in my mind and I withdrew both from it and my parents. I wanted to be by myself.

At the beginning I said I was uncertain whether this story would be funny or sad. Don't be in any doubt that at this moment I felt sad and isolated. It wasn't just that I had lost a friend whose memory could be stored away among my experiences. *What* I had lost took shape like something you suddenly see when you are looking at clouds. I couldn't arrange my thoughts of Dunkie like words cunningly assembled in a poem. There were too many of them. They swamped me. What would he have been like? What would have become of us? Duncan had been the only person I knew who sought me out. Doesn't that sound silly? The only person who ever came looking for me, not once but again and again.

I was setting the table a couple of days after the funeral. My mind was only half on the job and I had put the knives and forks the wrong way round. My mother wandered past and said casually, 'That's not the proper way to do it, Robbie.' She placed them correctly, then went on with whatever she had been doing. Straight away Dunkie's squeaky, half-broken voice said in my ear, 'I thought I ought to tell you. I thought it's the proper thing to do.' Not much more than two years before when poor, gawky Dunkie had been trying to put things right, when he was doing his gallant best to be a gentleman and cope with the situation his sister's machinations had dumped him in. All his short life he had tried to do things properly, and he was just beginning to get the hang of it when it all ended.

Dunkie's concern for consequences and doing things right hadn't been worth a damn when it really mattered. There he was, driving like the angels, and for all his pains he ended up joining them. I could not write it off as bad luck. I was not interested in the odds involved. What I felt like doing was exacting vengeance on someone or something. I began displaying a reckless disregard for consequences. I knew what I was doing, of course, and in a strange way that made me angrier still, because I could not bring myself to simply scream and curse and get it over with.

My first victims were my poor suffering teachers, who were not quite sure what had hit them. My years in the third and fourth forms had been marked by excellent academic achievement, coupled with a retiring social nature. In other words, I tended to keep to myself and was known for my reluctance to join in. My reports had never probed much deeper than that, noting in my younger years that I was 'not a good mixer', and when I arrived at secondary school that I did 'not function well in a group'.

The reason for this was that I had long ago latched on to the dynamics of class-room group work and its pitfalls. The theory was that all the busy little bees would contribute their bit to the task at hand and share in the intellectual ferment and excitement of producing whatever it was they were creating. I quickly discovered that all too often the ferment was confined to me, while my co-workers gossiped about their plans for next weekend, or conducted a post-mortem on the previous one. During my third form year I once provided the entire front page for a class-room newspaper single-handedly. After that I decided the time had come to adapt. From then on I chose my companions with care, but if I found myself in the company of clods, sluggards, or gigglers I would retreat into doodling silence. Perceptive teachers slipped me among the more diligent of my peer group. The rest left me to my own devices, noting my antisocial behaviour, but because I compensated in other ways no one ever marked me down as something sinister.

But in those early weeks of my seventh form year my behaviour lurched sharply towards the ominous. It began almost by accident one morning when I was late for a history period. I had quite genuinely forgotten the time. I was sitting in the library reading and brooding, completely oblivious to the bell signalling the change-over of periods. I came back to the here and now ten minutes after the period started and with a sense of shock hurried off to the room I was supposed to be sitting in. Then as I drew close I slowed to a relaxed walk and asked myself why on earth I should be worried about being ten minutes late.

My history teacher was a stern gentleman called Mr Ratcliffe to whom rules were rules. He operated according to the book. 'Why are you late, Robyn?'

If I had told him the real reason he would have accepted it with a long-suffering sigh, and that would have been that because it was the first time that I had ever been guilty of this misdemeanour. But I couldn't be bothered watching another of Mr Ratcliffe's long-suffering sighs, so on an impulse I said, 'I've been seeing Mr Bolton.'

'Do you have a late note?'

'No.'

'Well, off you go and get one.'

I executed a graceful exit. Mr Bolton was the Senior Dean. He frequently saw senior students to discuss problems, progress, complaints, and matters of that ilk, so my excuse was plausible. Most teachers would have accepted it from a seventh former and left it at that — but not Mr Ratcliffe. So off I sauntered to the Bolt Hole, which was Mr Bolton's office in the Senior Block, down the corridor from the senior common room. How I was going to handle this predicament bothered me not at all. I felt exhilarated by the faint whiff of danger and the need to improvise quickly.

Mr Bolton's office was empty. He must be teaching. I proceeded further down the corridor to his classroom, knocked and entered.

'Yes Robbie?' says he, turning from the blackboard.

My big moment. 'Mr Kray said you wanted to see me.' Mr Kray was the Deputy Principal. I'm almost ashamed to tell you that he was known as Fish.

Mr Bolton raised his eyebrows. 'That's news to me. He must have confused you with someone else.'

He returned to the blackboard and I wheeled back towards the door, but stopped short in a most convincing display of having just been struck by a sudden thought. 'Oh, I've got Mr Ratcliffe this period,' I said. 'I'll need a late note.'

Mr Bolton gave me an understanding smile and quickly scribbled on a piece of paper, 'Robbie left me at 11.40 a.m.,' signing his name at the bottom. I strolled back to my history room in an easy frame of mind. With official documentation a wandering pupil was absolutely safe from anything or anyone. Obviously there was one small flaw in my piece of paper and Ratty Baby could be guaranteed to pick it.

'This says you left Mr Bolton at 11.40. If you'd been seeing him at the start of the period you would have left him no later than 11.30.'

'Oh?' I said, bewildered innocence breaking out all over my face. 'He must have made a mistake. I know! He put down the time I've just left him — I mean the time when I went back to him just now — to get the note saying what time I'd left him before. He was teaching and he must have been busy — just now I mean — probably catching up because of the time he missed when I saw him before.' The wrinkles round Mr Ratcliffe's eyes began to furrow — a sure sign that he was getting rapidly fed up. I pressed home my advantage. 'Shall I go back for another note?'

'No,' he said despairingly, 'just sit down and let's get on with some notes.'

Naturally, this whole performance could have been blown apart through the suspicious Mr Ratcliffe asking a leading question of Mr Bolton in the staff room and following the trail of incriminating clues from there, but I knew this was unlikely to happen. Even Mr Ratcliffe was not that fanatical. To expose the heinous crime of Robbie Kemp evading the truth concerning the matter of her being late for a history class would have entailed assembling Messrs Bolton, Kray, and Ratcliffe in the one place at the same time to cross-check her story, and there was no way they were going to do that because it was not worth the trouble.

I had watched some of my fellow pupils doing this sort of thing for years. A few of them made a career out of it. But this was the first time I had found myself weaving a plot, and it had all happened because suddenly I couldn't be bothered. All at once I couldn't be bothered with a little lecture from Mr Ratcliffe about remembering the time.

I had learned to cope with most feelings and emotions of growing up, but this was my first real encounter with the seductive and alluring potion called apathy — a feeling that nothing you did mattered very much. I was surrounded by people exhorting me to prepare for an unknown future and endure the effort and anxieties that went with it because of the rewards to come. What happened if you didn't strive? What happened if you drifted into a kind of living sleep? All I knew was that my trivial encounter with Mr Ratcliffe left me with a peculiar sense of contentment. I did not feel triumphant at having won a silly game; I felt tranquillized.

That night I failed to do a history homework assignment. Next morning Mr Ratcliffe asked the reason. I told him that there was no reason. He muttered something about the consequences of slipping behind in this particular unit of work, which was very important, and left me alone. During the same week I failed to meet a deadline for a geography essay and neglected a language exercise for English. My teachers warned me of the consequences of falling behind. For my part I said nothing, thinking they might not share my newly discovered pleasure in open-eyed drowsiness — the lingering half-awake sensation before real sleep claims you, and you can forget everything.

I was careful not to reach the stage where they would snarl at me. I sensed a borderline which they would allow me to approach, but not cross without a baring of teeth and solitary conversations in the dens of Deans and Counsellors, being passed from one to the other accompanied by an escort of official reports — a lingering death, suffocated by sympathetic conversations. I found that judicious use of study periods was sufficient to produce some semblance of work. 'So long as you make an effort,' they would chant, leaving the unspoken consequence hanging in the air. 'So long as you make an effort!'

The trouble was, no one would stand up and let me fight them. I needed someone to batter my head against, but no one would oblige. They were all so damned understanding, and I was afraid to push too hard against people I knew or people I loved for fear that I would take one step too many and go beyond a point of retreat.

My parents were least use of all. They simply let me be. They met my every wish and accommodated their lives to meet my whims and fancies. On one occasion my mother even abandoned a particularly fruitful fishing trip, all because I said that I was bored trundling around in circles on the lake and wanted to go home — and this on a glorious morning off the mouth of the Waitahanui, with prime fish queuing up to leap on mother's favourite cobra lure as though they had formed a death pact. But all she said was, 'Yes, I think there might be a southerly blowing up. I think it might be a good idea to make for home.'

I was furious with her. Why did she let me get away with it? Why didn't she tell me to sit in the cabin and count matches if I felt bored? I knew the reason, of course. I was reminded of it every time I thought of Dunkie's face — and that made me feel guilty at putting on such a childish display, which in turn fed my sullen anger even further. What right did she have to side-step a blazing row with me? My father's silence I could understand. He had unknowingly wounded me far in the past, and nothing in the world could persuade him to pick and prod at that old scar by arousing anger between us.

No one was to blame. How could you blame anyone for the stew of contradictions that bubbled away in me at that time? All I wanted was the security of knowing that no matter what I did or said, no matter how eccentric or antisocial I became, sooner or later there would be someone there to blow the whistle on me and give me the comfort of self-righteous anger, a sense of relief that it was all over, that I had run up against someone who said, 'Stop! Enough!' There was a distinct lack of volunteers for the job. I was left to roam free in this rather dangerous state, vulnerable to anyone who might tempt me up pathways where recklessness could become a way of life.

At this point, dear old Stanley made his presence felt. He floated forward in a new role like a scarred, silver-haired old genie, trailing poisonous fumes as he emerged further from his ancient, crud-encrusted bottle. To cut short the imagery, he offered to show me what he kept in his aquarium, and who could refuse an offer like that?

IX
FISH TANKS

'Stanley and I were so sorry to read about the death of your friend,' said Mrs Swinton when I returned to my lawn-mowing duties. I had stayed away for two or three weeks and even thought of giving up the job altogether. I passed through a phase of wanting to avoid places where Dunkie had been part of the scenery, imagining that I would be unable to be there without recreating him in my mind.

Elizabeth Amelia put me right as soon as we resumed our after-work refreshments. 'Whatever you do,' she said, as she pumped vigorously at her spinning-wheel, 'don't try to put him out of your mind. Keep photographs of him around you. Look at him often. That way he will never seem far away.'

'But what about Cecilia?'

'Cecilia? Why are there no photographs of Cecilia on the wall?' She was silent and seemed to be choosing her words carefully as the spinning-wheel whirred. When they came they were an anticlimax. 'Let's just say that's another story,' she said. 'One day you might hear it.'

At least she hadn't advised me to pull myself together or told me that I would feel better as time passed. Nor did Stanley. I found his reaction to me puzzling. He smiled at me often, almost ingratiatingly, and was very helpful and solicitous. I would find him suddenly appearing at my side when the catcher needed emptying, whisking it away before I had a chance to say anything. He would insist on pushing the mower up the slope to return it to the garage. Most interesting of all, he began asking me to weed around some of his prize herb plants, even allowing me to pull away dead twigs and leaves from the plants themselves.

I decided that it was his way of showing tenderness and disguising a change in the way he regarded me. I doubted that he was trying to conceal anything. I suspected that he was unable to speak his feelings openly. Once or twice he walked over and sat near me when I stopped work for a rest under the shade of the trees. The burning hot days of late February and early March had arrived. The whole central plateau baked, and bronze haze drifted up from the horizon like a smoking halo. Even the edges of Stanley's tiny forest took on the appearance of savannah as the lawns began to dry and the sprinkler fought to keep the shallow rooted shrubs moist. Powdery pumice dust clogged the leaves within hours of the water being turned off. But further down the slope the taller trees reached deeper into the earth and under their branches the air was cool and the humus still faintly damp. Down there even the mosses and ferns kept their greenness and moisture.

One hot morning Stanley said to me, 'You can hardly see where we cut down that branch.'

'Which branch?'

'The one we cut down by the fence. Come and look.'

I followed him through the tall trees. He pointed to the new season's foliage which had spread across the gap where the overhanging branch had been lopped off. 'I hate cutting branches,' he said, 'but at least I always know that the tree will heal itself.'

'How tall will these trees grow?'

'Not much further. There isn't enough rain.'

'Why don't you put some fertiliser around them?'

'That wouldn't help much. You need endless water to grow a real forest.'

We moved out towards open daylight. He had come close to talking freely once or twice before, but had always pulled himself up short. This time I stayed quiet, but walked with him. I was rewarded.

'Are you interested in forests, Robbie?'

'I like yours.'

'Do you really?' He gave me a smile of genuine warmth. 'I'm glad to hear that. Not many people share my enthusiasm.' We had reached the edge of the lawn. 'Would you like a beer before you go? Are you allowed to drink beer? A lager perhaps?'

'That would be nice,' I said.

He strode up to the house and returned a couple of minutes later with two cans fresh from the fridge. He sat beside me slowly drinking and I thought he might have run out of words for the morning. Then he said, 'The interesting thing is that the great rain forests grow in soil that is almost as barren as a desert. Can you believe that?'

'I didn't know that,' I said, though he'd mentioned it to me once before. I felt uncomfortable, similar to the way I reacted to people who knocked at the door preaching those religions that are forever seeking converts.

'Not many people do,' he said. Then he seemed to come to a decision and he launched himself into conversation. 'I'll give you an interesting example. In the Amazon Basin the forests grow in ground that is like a wet sponge, from the Mato Grosso in the south right up to the Guianas in the north — though I think they call them something different these days. Who cares? The trees were there before man invented himself, and they'll be there long after the last politician who tries to change names on a map. In some parts of the rain forest there are rivers in which black water flows. Can you imagine that? I'll tell you why.

'They flow over ground that is nothing more than rock covered with a layer of rotting humus. Everything has been leached out of it. Everything! Every particle of soil. The water is stained by the juices seeping out of the humus. Yet the trees grow up like towers and pillars in great green cathedrals, and the rivers flow among them like great broad avenues of water. There are places where you can stand on one bank and not be able to see the other.'

He stopped and swallowed from his can. I wanted him to keep going. 'It must be strange walking in a forest like that.'

'Yes,' he said, 'but not difficult. That's the amazing thing about the primeval forest. It is not an impenetrable jungle. You don't hack your way through it with a machete. The canopies of the great trees shut out the sun, you see? If plants want the sun they must climb for it. They snake their way up the trunks and hang from the branches. The forest floor is all but bare except for the rotting trunks of those that have fallen, and the huge buttress roots springing from the trunks, and the tender plants that love the darkness and gloom. It's like walking in a great cathedral.'

'You said that before.'

'What do you mean? Said what?'

'You used the word "cathedral" before.'

'I suppose I did. I'm not the first. Many travellers in the Amazon have had that feeling, the sensation that they were walking in the midst of the mightiest creation on earth. You find most of them speaking of the grandeur of it.'

I recalled something else he had once touched on. 'And the danger?' I said.

He looked at me sharply. I was startled at the sudden intensity of his gaze. In an instant he was transformed from a garrulous old gentleman reminiscing about past experiences to someone sensing attack. 'What do you mean by that?'

I could not meet his stare. I shrugged. 'I just meant that you often read about dangerous animals and things in the Amazon — jaguars, anacondas, and so on.'

'What else?'

'What do you mean?'

'What else? What else have you read about living in the Amazon?'

'Well, there are the —'

'No!' he said abruptly. 'Don't say anything more.' He still stared at me, but his gaze had softened and his mouth twisted into a strange smile. 'Would you like me to show you something? Something you'll have to keep a secret?'

Dear Lord, I thought, as my sense of the ridiculous reappeared after a long absence, Stanley's a secret flasher about to come out of the closet! I composed myself. 'I can keep a secret,' I said, 'if that's what's worrying you.'

'Would you like to see inside my aquarium?'

Would I what! Careful, Robbie, don't frighten him off. 'I think that would be a great idea,' I said with a grin. 'If Dunkie had had his way he would have broken into it long ago.'

'Yes, I'd noticed his interest on more than one occasion,' Stanley said. 'As a matter of fact I rather enjoyed it. I always planned to let you in on the secret one day, but first you had to serve your apprenticeship.' By this time we had walked to the door of the small building butting on to the fence, and Stanley was fumbling among a bunch of keys. 'I had to be sure that you would appreciate what you are going to see. Do you understand what I mean?'

I didn't altogether, but I wasn't going to tell him that. 'It's something that's important to you,' I said, choosing a bland comment that seemed to fit the solemnity of the occasion.

'Exactly!' he replied. 'Something I'm proud of — something I don't want people to laugh about and treat as a big joke. I don't think you will,' he added, looking down at me. 'Not anymore.'

I was beginning to wonder whether I was about to see a troupe of performing eels balancing balls on their noses. He was talking like some self-important business tycoon about to reveal the secret of playing the perfect hand in Happy Families, while his mates were heavily into blackjack or poker.

The door swung open and he stepped aside to let me enter. At first I felt disappointed. The walls were lined with small tanks on metal shelves that stretched from the floor in three layers, reaching shoulder height. There must have been about fifty or sixty containers altogether, each about three-quarters full of water, and each with a slim plastic hose under the surface from which air bubbled. The small hoses slithered from each tank. They were joined to larger ones that wound their way around the lips of the shelves until they all met at a larger section beside the door, which was swallowed by a regulator attached to a large cylinder. I guessed that it contained compressed air.

There was a jumble of other fittings and pipes which I vaguely heard him describing, but I only half-listened as he muttered about filtration and water temperature. He was obviously proud of his apparatus, but it didn't interest me. After my initial regret at not seeing some glamorous creature of the depths imprisoned in the small room, I looked closely at what was there. I felt my skin beginning to chill.

If I had seen just a few of them, I doubt if I would have felt anything. But each tank contained one or two fish. They were unlike anything I had ever seen and they all seemed to be staring out through their glass walls, their fins gently moving as they glared at me. I felt as though I were on display and they were the spectators. At arm's length from me wherever I turned was an array of the cruellest mouths I have ever seen, some of them opening and closing to show teeth like those of an animal. They were sharp and pointed and arranged in even rows, bared and ready to chew. Their heads were like flattened snouts, tinged a reddish colour around the glossy smooth jowls. The red colour deepened along the lower half of their flat, squat bodies. The upper half was almost black, rising to a slight hump above the head as though a tensed muscle were about to exert its strength. The dorsal fin lay well back along the body, angled backwards. Large black dots were scattered over their scales, with a sprinkling of smaller white ones showing on the upper half.

The longer I stared at them, the more I felt they were going to charge and I had to fight a sudden urge to retreat to the sunlight. I breathed deeply and slowly mastered my shock. I glanced at Stanley. He was amused.

'They're no joke are they?' he said. 'Not when you see them all together. I can guess what you are feeling. I feel the same way myself sometimes when I'm in here alone with them, even after all these years.'

'What are they?' I whispered.

'Can't you guess? What else have you read about in the Amazon that are dangerous?'

'They can't be,' I muttered.

He almost giggled with glee. 'Oh, but they are, they are! They're piranha! They are real piranha. They are prime specimens of *Rooseveltiella nattereri*, the most feared subgroup of the piranha family!' He finished his announcement like a ringmaster introducing the star act of the show. 'They are very dangerous,' he said in a quieter voice. 'They are very dangerous indeed.'

A narrow bench stood in the middle of the room.

I levered myself up and sat there looking around me. One piranha, I could have coped with, even two or three, but seeing fifty or sixty of them *en masse* in their glass cells unnerved me. I felt claustrophobic, as though I were about to be enveloped by them. But after a while they began to look more placid. I found that I had dug my finger-nails into the palms of my hands and let them slowly relax.

'I've amazed you, haven't I?' said Stanley with a satisfied smile.

I yelped with laughter. 'Amazed me? You've astounded me! You've almost scared me out of my wits!'

'I suppose they could have that effect if you weren't used to them.'

'Where did they come from? How did you get them here?'

'That's an interesting story which I might tell you some day.' He said it in a way which left me in no doubt that he would keep his word, but I also sensed that he was getting a great kick out of all this and wanted to spin out his pleasure for as long as possible. A little bit of the big secret at a time for you, Miss Kemp — be patient and I might give you another morsel next time.

'You feed them on raw meat, don't you?'

'How did you know that?'

'We saw you bringing down the plastic container. We found a piece of meat outside the door one day.'

'Yes, I feed them meat as part of their diet, but they need supplements as well.'

'And when you feed them,' I continued, 'do they thrash around?'

'I don't understand.'

I told him, rather sheepishly, how Dunkie and I had listened outside the door one day just after he had left the aquarium. 'We heard the water churning around. Duncan thought you must be keeping something really huge in here.'

'Now I understand,' he said. 'No, that doesn't happen when I feed them exactly, but it's an interesting spectacle. I might show you one day, but not now.' He brought his hands together and smiled with satisfaction. 'I think you've seen enough for one day, haven't you? I've work to do, even if you've finished. Oh, I nearly forgot. It's pay-day isn't it?' He fished into his pocket and drew out some notes. 'Here you are. There's a little extra as a bonus for excellence. I'm in a good mood today.'

He was too. He almost bounded outside and I actually heard him whistling as he strode away. Then he stopped and turned back. 'Just one thing, Robbie. You will remember that this is a secret between us won't you?'

I grinned back and nodded. 'Of course I will. You can trust me.' I felt strangely warm towards him, something I had never imagined could ever happen. I was glad to see him get such pleasure out of showing me his little pets. I understood, too, that when it came to recklessness I might have stumbled on someone who was in a league of his own. I'd heard of people who allowed pet snakes to have the run of the house, but here was someone with real class. Who could have imagined what Stanley kept locked up at the bottom of his garden?

I was still chuckling as I walked through the garage and out on to the driveway. I was in time to see Mrs Swinton drive through the gate and stop by the front door. She began struggling out of the front seat, laden with paper bags and parcels with a couple of letters perched precariously on top.

When she saw me she smiled. 'You're looking much happier today, Robbie. What's amusing you?'

'Yes, I think I am feeling better,' I said. 'Here, let

me help you with that.' One of the parcels had tipped as she edged herself out, and the envelopes fluttered to the ground. They were aerogrammes. I picked them up and poked them into the top of the bag of apples which Elizabeth Amelia gratefully passed to me.

When we had shared out everything she said, 'So what's happened to cheer you up?'

'Mr Swinton has just shown me his aquarium.'

Her head snapped round and she stared at me. 'He's shown you inside?' she asked sharply.

'Yes,' I said.

'He's shown you the fish? He's told you what they are?'

'Yes, he has. Why? Has he done something wrong?'

She tried to recover herself and forced her voice to be casual. 'No, no, of course not my dear. It's just that I never expected him ever to show the fish to anyone. They've always been a kind of secret — something he's always kept to himself.' Her face brightened. 'You're privileged. Come in for a moment. If I don't put these parcels down they'll scatter everywhere.'

I followed her through the back door into the kitchen. She collapsed in relief against the bench and allowed her purchases to slide across its surface. 'That's better,' she said, her back to me. 'Would you like some coffee?'

'Not today thanks. I'm running late.'

She turned to face me. She was worried again. 'You said that he told you what those fish are.'

'Yes, he said they were piranha.'

'Piranha, yes. Do you know what piranha are, Robbie? Do you know where they come from?'

'Of course I do, though I didn't know which variety these ones were. I suppose I imagined they were all the same. He didn't tell me how he got them, but

I think I can see why he likes them. He seems to have spent a bit of time in the Amazon from the way he was talking. I suppose they're a kind of souvenir. I suppose you must have been there too.'

Elizabeth Amelia did not respond to my bright smile and my flagrant hint. She began fussing around her paper bags, unpacking groceries. 'Oh yes, it's quite a story,' she said, 'but like you I'm running a bit late. Some other time?'

'That's OK,' I chirped. 'I'll see you next week.'

'Robbie! You do realize that it's not altogether legal to be keeping fish like that don't you?'

'Of course. Don't worry, I told Mr Swinton I could keep a secret.'

'I'm sure you can. I'm sure he wouldn't have shown you unless he thought he could trust you. But I thought I should remind you. There could be serious trouble if anyone found out. Just one slip of the tongue. . . .'

'It's all right,' I said. 'Believe me, I wouldn't dream of telling a soul. I wouldn't want to. I love the thought of my being the only one who knows, apart from you and Mr Swinton. It's just — just marvellous!'

I finally forced a genuine laugh out of Elizabeth Amelia. 'All right,' she said, 'I believe you. Off you go.'

For some reason I felt almost as exhilarated as I had on the day when I had landed the lawn-mowing job. I did a running leap into the saddle of my ten-speed and free-wheeled down the road. I waved to the postie who was sweating up the hill, shoving her heavily laden bike. I had turned the corner at the bottom before something clicked.

If that was the postie making her weary way up towards the Swinton residence, where had Elizabeth Amelia acquired those two aerogrammes I had retrieved for her? Then an old habit came to my aid. Ever since

I can remember I have never been able to pick up an envelope, whether intended for me or not, without glancing at the address. It is almost like an intuitive reaction with me. I have a quick look, then instantly forget it. Only this time the address on those two aerogrammes had flashed across my trusty retinas recently enough to have lingered. They read,

Mrs E.A. Swinton,
P.O. Box 2671,
Taupo,
New Zealand.

How very puzzling. I couldn't be certain that I had the numerals correct, but it was definitely a post office box number. Did sly old Elizabeth Amelia have her own private postal service that bypassed the regular door-to-door delivery? I wondered if Stanley ever saw those letters, or whether his artful little wife had a fragment of existence he knew nothing about. It was the kind of bonus I needed to round off a glorious morning and I rode home feeling completely invigorated, as though I was once again stirring into life.

X
FEEDING TIME

For the first time in weeks I walked into the house without dreading the prospect of talking to my parents, and trying to find a hidden motive behind everything they said to me. For their part, I'm sure they were relieved at being able to open their mouths without having their most innocent remarks analysed for their significance. Poor old Mum had even become reluctant to ask me something as simple as, 'Would you like a cup of tea?' in case I demanded to know why she thought I needed one. So when I breezed in that morning and said 'Hi!' and asked if *she'd* like a cup of tea, I could almost hear her breathe a sigh of relief. Her Robbie was becoming her old self again, and as far as Mum needed to know, I suppose I was.

There was no doubting her delight. When she thought I was out of earshot I overheard her say to Dad, 'I think Robbie's snapping out of it at last. She was almost her old self when she came home this morning.'

'Robbie will never be her old self again,' Dad said.

'She seemed cheerful enough.'

'That's not necessarily the same thing,' he replied, 'but I don't suppose it matters much so long as she's finding things a bit easier.'

There was a pause, then my mother said, 'I hadn't realized that she and Duncan were that close.'

'I don't think that's the point — how close they were, I mean. Robbie's always been a self-contained sort of person. I think she's imagined up till now that she'll never need anything more than herself, and she's just discovered how wrong she was.'

'She's more like you than me, isn't she?' my mother said.

'I suppose she is. So I guess we're both lucky we've got you. You think I sorted things out for myself when Robert died — but I didn't.'

'But what about Robbie? She'll be all right won't she?'

Before he could reply I began to move away, and my foot scuffed on the floor. When he did speak I could swear his voice was raised slightly. 'Don't worry. She knows we're here if she wants us.' I'm certain he knew I was listening and wanted to make sure I heard.

My father is a shrewd old devil. I have never been able to decide whether he did me a service or an injury by staying politely on the edges of my life. He never put himself out to enquire closely into what I was thinking or doing. He always responded to anything I asked him and was as dutiful as they come, but he valued his private world and his secret ambitions. Since those years I have come to realize that he knew more about me than I suspected then, and that he wanted to keep me away from his shadow. He was a person who never stood still, never content to repeat things he had done before. It must have been about this time that he began carving pumice sculptures for display — large semi-abstract works that have since found their way to sites at several prominent places around the town. But I didn't notice this change in his work as he hacked and rasped in the garage. I had piranha on my mind.

I found nothing about them in the school library apart from a few mentions in a couple of encyclopaedias. These were dull because they all went to great pains to point out how travellers' tales about the vicious predatory habits of these fish were greatly exaggerated. I have always found the bland, neutral entries one finds in encyclopaedias to be thoroughly maddening, written by a collection of solemn scholars jostling for a part of the fence to park their bums on.

The public library had more of the same, so I decided to shoot for the top and filled in an inter-loan card requesting information from the National Library no less. A week later I was rewarded. A large envelope arrived with four pages photocopied from what seemed to be an elderly book on the subject of the fishes of western South America. There was no indication as to who wrote it, or when, but I judged it to be venerable from its unfashionably large page size, together with the author's habit of never referring to anything published later than 1920.

Whoever the author was, he had me hooked from the opening paragraph:

> The members of this subfamily constitute the infamous tribe of 'man-eaters' known in the Guianas as the *perai, piraya* and *caribe,* in Brazil as the *piranha* (pronounced peer-ahn²-yah) and in the Oriente of Peru as *paña* (pronounced pahn²-yah). They are most frequently taken in the clearer waters of the quieter, back-water bayous and their inlets and outlets, and less abundantly in the swifter and muddier waters. They, together with the caymans and such fishes as *Roeboides,* make set-net fishing impossible. Some of my gill-nets were destroyed the very first time they were placed in the water.

There, in good old-fashioned prose that stepped from line to line like a stately matron, was the kind of stuff I wanted to hear. Anyone who can come straight to the point and tell us we are dealing with an infamous tribe of man-eaters is never going to be condemned to write encyclopaedia articles. Having cleared his throat in his opening paragraph, my anonymous oracle proceeded to relate a string of stirring anecdotes to prove his case that *Rooseveltiella nattereri* is not a fish you keep in the same pond as goldfish. I underlined the bits that caught my attention and reproduce some of them here in case you ever want to have a bad dream about exploring the Amazon.

> It is necessary to fish with large hooks, for otherwise the paña will either bite your line, your leader, or your hook in two as part of the day's work. Hooks lost and leaders bitten off were the rule rather than the exception.

If you are a decent, law-abiding citizen in the jungle, it pays to watch your step: 'Schomburgk tells of seeing three young capybara with toes amputated by the fish, and waterfowl walking about on stumps of feet.'

Man himself has featured more than once on the piranha hit list: 'The well-known Colonel Rondon lost a toe to one of them.' (Personally, I'd never heard of the Colonel, but I didn't begrudge him his place in history.) 'Many Indians are seen with the extremities of fingers and toes missing. Miller relates the loss of a piece of finger while washing the blood of a specimen from his hands at the water's edge.' Then there is the tale of the unfortunate Mrs S: 'The latter, while idly dangling her hand overboard in a canoe, thought one of the oarsmen had struck her with his paddle. She began to rebuke him for his awkwardness when she discovered that her finger was gone.' (I like to think that she was trying to point the missing digit accusingly at the time.)

But if you know the territory you can be safe:

> Miller tells of a native who, in fishing for piranha, dropped his purse overboard among them. By

wading cautiously from shore without agitating the water, he recovered the purse with his feet and was not molested. Other observers report that the tribesmen of the forest know where, and under what circumstances, it is safe to enter streams without fear of lurking piranha, although known to be near at hand.

(Right! You make damned sure you're carrying the proper accessories!)

Then came the tales of wholesale slaughter: 'McGovern relates an observation: a sheep carcass was completely consumed in two and one-half minutes. Im Thrm knew personally several cases of drownings in which only the bones of victims were discovered after more or less immediate search.' Then there is this remarkable anecdote: 'Hartt tells of a half-wit who, sitting on a river-bank, was frightened by the discharge of a cannon, fell into the water, and parts of whom were discovered in the stomach of piranha next day.' (I hope the incompetent idiot who set up his cannon on the river bank next to the hapless half-wit was duly court-martialled!)

But I must not leave you with the impression that the piranha is without its uses:

That such predators, whose extreme vigour and rapacity are expressed even in line and colour, should be useful to man does not seem credible. But as a matter of fact they are rather favourite food fishes in many sections, and their provocative temperaments make them especially easy to take.

I found all this very stimulating reading and could hardly wait to show off my newly discovered knowledge to Stanley. I suppose I thought he would be as entertained as I had been. After all, you could hardly read some of those yarns without smiling. It was the stuff of fantasy, not far removed from the visions of scantily clad Amazons that have pranced across the pages of jungle comics since someone resurrected the legends of female warriors from the journal of an eighteenth century explorer. But Stanley was not amused. He looked at me very coolly and said, 'You're right to be sceptical about some things you read, Robbie, but don't confuse the strange and unusual with fantasy. These little beauties can do things you could barely imagine.'

We were standing in the aquarium hut, where I was now a welcome visitor. I had been trying to get across to him the quaintness of the stories, rather than disbelief in them, but I didn't express myself very well. I could see that I had affronted him and for one agonising moment I thought he was going to banish me forever from his roomful of pets.

Then his eyes glinted. 'I think it's time you learned more about my piranha. It's not time for their regular feed, but a morning snack won't harm them, just this once. You wait here.' He marched out the door, up towards the house. He reappeared a few minutes later carrying his plastic ice-cream container which he placed on the bench. It was about half full of chunks of meat. He picked these out carefully placing them on a sheet of newspaper. When he had finished, the bottom of the container held blood, about a centimetre deep. 'I always like the blood to drain out of the meat,' he said. 'It helps to liven up the feeding ritual.'

I began to feel icy fingers creeping up my back. He still had that glint in his eyes and I had a feeling that I was about to witness something that Stanley did not intend that I should forget.

'Now!' he said in a very business-like fashion. 'You

mentioned something about piranha snapping off hooks, as I recall.'

I nodded, adopting a watch and listen policy.

He tugged open a large drawer that I had not noticed before, fitted underneath the bench. He rummaged around and produced a small nail. 'I don't have a hook on the premises, but this will do as well.' He tied a piece of string around the head of the nail then pushed the point through a chunk of meat. 'Let's see what happens,' he said.

Stanley went to one of the tanks on the upper layer and raised his arm so that the baited nail swung back and forth over the surface of the water. The fish inside barely moved, but stared stolidly at us. He quickly dipped the nail beneath the water behind the fish and withdrew it swiftly. I saw a swirl of water and the piranha darted about as though being jerked from side to side. 'That was just to warm him up,' Stanley said. He lowered the nail again and let it stay there. Another swirl, and the nail was bare. 'Not quite, but you can see the bare metal where his teeth marked it.' They were like gleaming scratches across the dull grey colour of the nail. 'The problem is, there's no barb so the meat slips off easily. Let's try again, but this time we'll tie it on.'

He speared another morsel of meat, but this time trussed it up tightly with a piece of string like a condemned man being bound to a stake. He lowered the nail. I barely had time to see what happened. It was engulfed in a flurry and froth of water and I saw a flash of silvery scales. Then he raised the nail, sheared cleanly in half.

Stanley was delighted. 'I've never done that before,' he said. 'I must remember that trick. I just hope he knows how to digest half a nail.' He chuckled. 'Now, what shall I show you next? How would you like to put your fingers into one of these tanks? Do you think that would be a good idea, Robbie?'

His voice had changed. It had lost its relaxed, confident tone and was becoming more strident. At the same time I could see that he was growing more absorbed in what he was doing. He was aware of my presence, but I could have been a stage prop.

'Well, what about it?' he said. 'Would you care to try?' He asked the question without looking at me. He was passing slowly in front of the tanks. He didn't want me to reply. He wanted to show me. Raising his hand to one of the tanks he said, 'We won't attempt it on the little darling we've just stirred up. Let's try this one. Now the important thing is to move your hand very slowly, and not disturb the water as you gradually dip it under — very slowly — like this.' As he spoke he let his hand ease down through the water's surface until it was submerged, with tiny bubbles of air rushing to cling to his skin. The piranha did not move. It stared at me, quietly moving its pectoral fins.

He withdrew his hand from the water. 'There you are! It can be done if you know how. Are you sure you wouldn't like to try?' I shook my head. 'One day you might. There's really no danger if you're careful. But now let me show you how to catch a piranha if you feel like fish for tea. Your stories were right — they make delicious eating. I'll tell you what we'll do. Let's catch the one with a half a nail in his belly! There's a chance he'll die of indigestion anyway.'

By this time Stanley was in full flight. He was hardly aware that I was there. I had backed away to the other side of the bench and stood near the door watching him as he darted about like a clockwork toy that has been wound up tight. He was talking to himself as much as to me and I could hear his breath hissing through his nostrils. He leered in my direction. 'How do we catch a piranha without using a fish hook? Easy. We tear off a piece of cloth, like this.' He reached under the bench and brought out the remains of an old pyjama jacket. He tore off the remnant of a sleeve. He had obviously done this more than once before. 'Now watch! Just watch this!'

I felt my stomach beginning to stir as he moved across to the plastic container and dipped the end of the flannelette cloth into the pool of blood at the bottom. 'The Indians in the Guianas sometimes use this trick,' he said as he prodded the cloth to soak it completely. 'They normally use blood from leeches,' he added conversationally, 'but this does just as well. Piranha can snap off hooks, but this method turns their most dangerous weapon back against them. Can you guess what I mean? Their teeth! Their mouths open and shut like jaws packed with razors, but sometimes their jaws get stuck.'

While he was chattering he was tying the dry end of the cloth to the end of a hearth broom handle which had appeared from somewhere. 'You can hold the end of the cloth in your fingers, but it's better to be safe. Now watch this!' He held the cloth over the tank of the fish that had already dined on meat and nail. A few drops of blood dripped into the water and broke into pink clouds. Instantly the fish burst into a frenzy and the tank swirled and churned in a flurry of bubbles. Then Stanley lowered the baited cloth into the water. I could see the broom handle quiver with the shock and Stanley tensed his wrists as the cloth was tugged up and down. He lifted it quickly from the water and moved over to the bench.

The piranha was dangling, flapping back and forth, its teeth firmly clenched to the fragment of Stanley's old pyjamas. The man himself almost cackled with delight. 'Got you!' he said. 'Got you! The poor devil can't let go! Do you see that? The teeth get entangled in the fabric and can't let go, and then you've got him!'

Well that's great Stanley, really marvellous, I thought. You've given a whole new meaning to blood sports. I watched as he laid the fish on the bench, where it flopped about, still gripping the cloth between its jaws. Then it began to grunt! I swear on my heart that I do not tell a lie. It actually grunted.

'They sometimes do that,' said Stanley calmly. He reached under the bench yet again, this time producing a knife from his magic drawer of tricks. 'They're still dangerous at this stage,' he said. 'This is the moment when fishermen in the Amazon lose toes, when they have live piranha kicking around in the bottom of the boat. Or sometimes a finger if they're not careful when they're picking them up. The cloth trick isn't widely used, but it does help in keeping the mouth of your catch fully occupied.'

His voice had grown quieter as he approached the fish with the knife. He seemed almost reluctant to put the fish to death. I knew I could not watch. I had witnessed the bludgeoning of countless trout, but this was too much. I opened the door and stepped outside, leaning against the frame and feeling the breeze on my face. Stanley prattled on, unaware that I wasn't watching. 'There we are!' he said. 'Safely dispatched. Shall I gut him now so we can have a look at the nail in his stomach?' He didn't wait for an answer. 'Perhaps not. I want to show you something else.'

I peeked back inside and saw him pick up the ice-cream container with its offering of blood, and I felt my own stomach heave.

Stanley continued his running commentary, completely oblivious to the effect his performance was having on me. 'Do you recall asking me about the water thrashing? About how you heard it through the door?

Well, this is how it's done. There's not enough blood to do them all — when there is, the effect is amazing. But you'll get the idea if I bait this row of tanks along the top. Are you watching? Here we go!' He was like an excited child setting his toy trains on a collision course, hardly able to wait for the crash.

I glanced back inside and saw him prance along the row of tanks tilting the container above the water. The tanks exploded into a bubbling eruption in succession like detonating firecrackers. I glimpsed pink froth foaming on the surface of each, then my whole body broke out in a layer of cold sweat and I knew I was going to faint if I stayed around much longer. I walked over to the nearest patch of shade and sat down, breathing deeply. Inside the hut, Stanley's voice droned on.

I forced myself to look at the trees, concentrating on the leaves, the bark, the flowers — or anything! A fantail hopped into view. I tried to guess where it would dart next. I was wrong. I guessed again. By the fourth guess I could feel the clammy chill leaving me and I began to breathe normally. I closed my eyes for a moment, then nearly leapt to my feet as I felt a hand on my shoulder and recognized Stanley's grimy fingers resting on my shirt. I was a second away from screaming 'Rape!' when I looked into his face.

Stanley's face was never an agreeable sight at the best of times, but now it verged on the grotesque. His mouth hung half open and his eyes seemed to have sagged so that he resembled a spaniel in mourning. My emotions did one of those roller-coaster swoops they seem to be afflicted with, and I nearly hooted with laughter. But I was brought up short by that look in his face, like someone pleading for mercy and understanding.

'I didn't mean to upset you,' he muttered. 'Believe

me, I didn't mean to upset you. I thought you were interested. From what you said to me about what you'd been reading I thought you would want to see. I'm sorry if I did the wrong thing.'

I tried to round up my thoughts and managed a feeble, 'That's OK.'

'I wouldn't want you to think that I was trying to scare you or anything.'

'It's all right,' I said. 'I suppose it was the shock of seeing it all at once.'

He managed a thin smile. 'Of seeing what they are really like?'

I took my cue. 'Yes, that's it,' I said. 'Seeing what they're really like.'

His smile broadened. I was aware of his hand still resting on my shoulder and that I wanted to be rid of it, preferably with a minimum of fuss. I let my body slump, as though I had suddenly felt a twinge in my back, neatly slid myself away from him and stood up, trying to be casual and relaxed. 'I really was interested.'

'Are you sure?'

'Yes, truly,' I said, with what I hoped was conviction.

'They really are fascinating creatures. I've been studying them for a long time. I bred them myself from my original stock. Would you like me to tell you about it?'

Actually I did, but not right then. I wanted to go home, but I knew I would have to execute my exit as gracefully as possible. Stanley was staring at me anxiously. 'Yes, I'd love to,' I said, 'but you'll have to wait for another day. I'll have to come back anyway to finish the lawns. Looking at piranha has held me up.'

He was still watching me closely. I sensed that if I gave the slightest sign of turning my back on him, he was going to shut himself away like a clam in a bank vault, and I didn't want that to happen. More of the real Stanley had eased into view and I wanted to see the rest. 'Look, I'll come up one day after school next week. Would that be all right?' I looked him straight in the eye.

He glanced away first. 'Of course,' he said. 'Come up whenever you like.'

I hadn't realized I had been holding my breath, and let it escape slowly as I strolled up the lawn. I wasn't sure what Stanley was thinking but he didn't know my real thoughts either. What I had witnessed that morning was like seeing the difference between a drawing in a comic as the hero is shot cleanly through the shoulder by a small black dot drawn on the page, and the reality of blood, shock, and shattered bone. The difference between the comfortable fantasy and the hands-on, violent reality. At the same time I suddenly appreciated the value of the fantasies we live by. Without them life would be full of tortures. I understood for the first time how some people could be reluctant to abandon their protection. Most important of all, I wondered where Stanley was living his life, because when I went over the events of that morning I concluded that it was Stanley Swinton's behaviour that had disturbed me even more than the primordial antics of *Rooseveltiella nattereri*.

XI
AMAZON TALES

More than once I had been on the point of talking to my father about Stanley. I had resisted the temptation, partly because I wanted to know more about his private aquarium. The other reason was the promise I had made to Elizabeth Amelia. She had as good as sworn me to secrecy, and I trusted her. She obviously knew what Stanley was up to and I felt confident that she was in control of the situation. Little did either of us know.

I almost returned to finish the lawns the following afternoon but, after careful thought, decided against it. I did not want Stanley to think I was over-eager to enter further into his bizarre world. I was not going to be a push-over. My pose would be one of cool detachment. I choose the word 'pose' with care, because whatever else might have changed in me, my old habit of creating theatre out of other people's thoughts had not diminished. If anything it had become more habitual since Dunkie's death, probably because my inner eye had been opened to a vast new wonderland of emotions.

In the case of Stanley Swinton, one important piece of evidence had presented itself as a result of that gory morning at the fishes' feeding trough. Stanley feared that I might go away forever. For some reason he was frightened of losing me. The memory of that pleading look on his scarred face as he sat beside me on the lawn was even more vivid than my recall of the piranha feeding-frenzy. I could not imagine at first what caused it. After all, there was nothing special to mark me out from a hundred girls my age. I was replaceable. Or was I? I remembered Elizabeth Amelia's comment about my astonishing resemblance to the long-gone Cecilia, and deep in my gut I knew I had hit pay dirt. Stanley's hand resting on my shoulder took on a whole new meaning. There was no question of the middle-aged cad seeking to 'take advantage of me', as they used to say in polite circles. My instinct told me that if anyone held an advantage it was me, since I was convinced I knew what he was feeling. (My God, I was innocent, but you must remember that I was but a cocky adolescent at the time!)

When I turned up at the Swintons a couple of days later I was watching and waiting. So was Stanley. I saw the curtains move at the front windows and glimpsed his silvery crew cut before he stepped back from the light. I quickly had the mower roaring and was into action before he could come near me. When he did appear I waved cheerfully, but smiled coolly, making clear to all the world that here was a young lady in complete command of her lawns. When I had finished I pushed the mower in a confident, sweeping curve to the front of the aquarium, revved the engine in a noisy salute and switched off.

I knew he was inside. I knocked boldly on the door, shoved it open and said, 'How are the fish today?' I could see at once from his face that Stanley had expected a much more hesitant and timorous Robbie, and my entrance disconcerted him. But not for long.

'Come in, come in!' he said with forced breeziness. 'I'm afraid there won't be much to see today. I don't like changing their routine too often, and they're not due for a meal.'

'Don't worry about it,' I said, 'I only want to look at them.' I moved slowly around the tanks inspecting the contents, thinking to myself, you sinister little specimens, enjoy life while you can. 'They really are fascinating creatures, aren't they?' I said. 'So beautifully built.'

'You've said it all,' said Stanley. 'So beautifully built for what they've been designed to do. You know, many people can't get out of the habit of judging wild creatures as though they were human. "Thou shalt not kill", the commandment says, and people seem to think that animals should have read the Bible too.'

(Yes, Stanley, it's called anthropomorphism, and I've learned about it in biology, and I still think your piranha are evil little bastards — pug-nosed Draculas with fins.)

I ambled to the doorway and sat down on the step, angling my legs across the exit so that Stanley could not walk out without making a deliberate effort. 'Don't mind me,' I said, 'you just get on with what you were doing while I cool down. The weather's still very warm isn't it? We often find autumn a long time coming in Taupo.'

I let him fuss round with some air tubes for a couple of minutes, then said, ever so innocently, 'You said once that you'd tell me where you got your fish from.' I picked up a piece of straw and chewed it, as though I couldn't have cared less what he answered.

'Did I really?' he said. 'I don't remember that.' He pretended to be puzzled.

'Oh well, never mind,' I said, moving as if I was about to stand up and go.

Stanley came to heel at once. 'Wait. Yes, now I remember. Well, why not. There's no harm in telling you.'

I felt very smug. I had him. What he feared most was my losing interest in him. He walked around the bench and sat on the floor with his back against the opposite door jamb. He stretched out his legs to that his feet disappeared from view somewhere underneath my arm-pit. As he began talking his knee moved over, ever so casually, to rest against my leg. I shifted it away without thinking anything of it at the time. In retrospect, Doctor Watson, it assumed greater significance.

'What would you like me to tell you?' Stanley asked. 'Where would you like me to begin?'

'I want to know how you got hold of those fish. You said the other day that you've been breeding them, so they can't be the ones you started with.'

'Indeed not, though I still have one or two of my originals.'

'And they would have come from South America. You've been to South America haven't you? You said as much.'

He nodded slowly. Then he rested his head against the door jamb, half-closing his eyes, and seemed to slip into a kind of reverie as he talked. 'They spawn much as other fish do. Sometimes you find their eggs in nests in depressions in the river sands, laid in a ball which would fit comfortably in your hand. I recall someone telling me of finding their eggs among the roots of lianas. The best place to look is in the backwater tributaries. Of course, the easiest way is to catch live specimens and get them to breed in aquarium tanks. The vital thing is to make sure you have running water circulating over them, and plenty of oxygen, and your water must be the right temperature. I had more than one failure before I succeeded.'

'How did you catch them?'

'With a hand net, baited with meat.'

'Wouldn't they have damaged the net?'

'Quite often, and then it was a matter of making repairs and trying again. But that wasn't the difficult part. The hard part of the operation was keeping them alive on the way down river.'

'In canoes?'

'Yes, but usually with the help of an outboard

motor on the back. Even in my time we rarely had to rely on paddlers, and of course today I would probably have used a helicopter. I wouldn't like that at all. In fact, I only put up with outboard engines because I had to — noisy damned things. If you really want to become part of the rain forest and feel its presence, there is nothing to equal drifting along a river close to the green walls listening to the silence all around you.'

(I nearly butted in to ask him why he chose to put up with a four-stroke motor mower in his private paradise if noise offended him so much. But I didn't. I probably had a private vision of my own, of me panting behind a hand mower.)

Stanley's voice flowed on. 'The silence is amazing. You can hear noises of course, but it's as though the whole jungle is walking on tiptoe, or cowering away from the sun, muffling every sound it is forced to utter. You are surrounded by life, but it hides away. Then at night you lie in your hammock and you hear the jungle come alive with the noise of monkeys, birds, toads, and all the creatures that live in trees, all signalling and calling to each other.

'You lie there getting used to it, sweltering with one leg dangling over the edge of the hammock trying to make the air stir. You slap at the whining mosquitoes, wondering why you ever left home. But you grow accustomed to it. People often think of the jungle as the home of dangerous animals, but do you know what you should fear most in the jungle? Not the jaguar. Not even the piranha, because at least you know where to expect him. But the insects! The ants! They can nearly drive you mad. I've seen an invasion of fire ants empty whole villages — their bite can be excruciating and they'll eat anything in sight. Have you heard about the army ant? They eat the flesh of anything they find in their path. They move in columns through the jungle with a faint, hissing noise. They can pass across the corpse of a small animal and leave nothing but a skeleton a few minutes later. Fantastic creatures!'

Stanley's devotion to the creatures of the Amazon seemed to wax and wane according to their ability and speed at consuming flesh. We were driving further and further away from piranha. 'How did you get them back here?' I said.

'What? Get what back here?'

'Your piranha. How did you get them from there to here?' It was like making a two-year-old eat another spoonful of veges. 'How did you bring them into the country?'

'I didn't bring them in as fish. They arrived here as fertilized eggs in a very large vacuum flask. They were in water of exactly the right temperature, and enough of them survived until I could get them into running water again.'

'A vacuum flask? You mean something like a big thermos flask?'

'That's correct.' He stared at me calmly. 'Why? Don't you believe me?'

'Of course,' I replied. 'After all, they're here aren't they? I was just thinking that you were very lucky to get them in. You arrived by air, I suppose.'

He nodded. 'In an ordinary commercial airliner.'

'You must admit that you were lucky to get a vacuum flask full of fertilized piranha eggs past Customs without someone asking to have a look inside.'

Stanley almost squirmed with satisfaction. 'But I was cunning! I gave them no reason to *want* to look inside. Who would want to inspect a brand-new vacuum flask still done up in its cellophane wrapping, being carried inside a plastic carrier bag from a duty free shop of a South American airport?' He sat back with a triumphant smile which said, 'Take that you sceptical little brat, and have faith in your elders.'

'You mean you bought a brand-new flask and removed it carefully from its wrappings?'

'Correct.'

'Then filled it with piranha eggs and water, and replaced it in its wrappings so that it looked as though it came fresh off the shelf?'

'Exactly. It wasn't too difficult. The tricky part of the operation was removing the cellophane without damaging it. To tell you the truth, I had to buy three flasks before I was completely successful. To this day there's probably some delighted rubbish collector in Rio de Janeiro still using a couple of vacuum flasks he discovered in mint condition one morning in a back alley waste bin.'

There were a few details in this story I would have liked to have questioned, but there was no denying that Stanley possessed a roomful of piranha. He must have got hold of them somehow. I let the matter of their acquisition rest.

'You said that you've been breeding them.'

'That was part of the plan,' he said casually.

Here we go, I thought. Stanley wants me to ask about his plan. For one mischievous moment I wondered what would happen if I were to say, 'Thank you very much for an interesting afternoon', and go home. But I played along. 'What was your plan? Have you been selling off your surplus stock to people who don't get kicks out of their goldfish anymore?'

As soon as I'd said it, I knew that I'd gone too far. Stanley's body tensed and his eyes narrowed. 'You can be very flippant, can't you, Robbie? I would hate to think you were laughing at me. You're not laughing at me are you?'

The flush that warmed up my cheeks was genuine embarrassment. More than this, his tone vaguely frightened me. 'No, no, sorry — it's just that I can't see why you would want to breed them unless you were selling them.'

He eased back against the door jamb. 'No, I don't suppose you could. I doubt if anyone could imagine why I would want to breed as many generations of fish as I could as fast as possible.'

'I'd like to know,' I said meekly.

He hesitated, then said, 'I've been carrying out an experiment in adaptation.'

What was I supposed to say to that? He obviously wanted me to ring his bell every time he paused before he'd feed me another morsel. 'What have you been adapting them to do?'

'Not to *do* anything. I have been slowly changing their environment, generation by generation. My aim has been to do without that.' He pointed to the thermal bore head in its concrete housing close to the door. Something Dunkie had once said popped into my head.

'You've succeeded, haven't you? Dunkie noticed it. I remember now. He said one day that you didn't seem to be using the bore anymore. He thought you'd been using it to heat the water in the aquarium and we couldn't figure out why you'd suddenly stopped.'

'It has taken me years,' said Stanley, 'but I think I've done it at last.' He waited for me to respond, but I had a feeling he wouldn't need any prompting this time. 'I can't be certain, but I think I have about twelve fish that can live comfortably in cold water. The rest of them still need help in winter and I have to take care to heat their tanks — but these twelve! They're the ones. They lasted all through last winter, and I'm sure they can do it!'

'Do what?'

'I'm sure they can survive happily in water with a temperature of ten degrees.'

108

'Ten degrees? Why ten, exactly?'

'Because that is the lowest temperature the water in the lake reaches. And I've tested them lower than that! I put ice-cubes in their tanks and brought the temperature down even lower. I lost more than half of them, but that didn't matter because I wanted to be sure. And these twelve survived!'

He was beginning to be obsessed with the sound of his own voice. He was fast becoming the self-hypnotized zombie he had been a couple of days before when he was giving me his live demonstration.

'Mr Swinton,' I said slowly and carefully, 'why is it important that you breed some piranha that can live in water temperatures of ten degrees — the temperature of the lake?'

'Why do you think?'

I knew what I thought, but I wanted to hear him say it. 'I can't imagine. I mean, they live in nice warm tanks in here — or they can if you let them.'

'That is true. But you see, I want to be prepared.'

'Prepared for what?'

'In case I ever decide it would be a good idea to stock the lake with some marine life that might add a little excitement to the life of this dull self-satisfied community of sleazy money-grubbers with their motels and launches and cars and glossy houses and all the rest of it!' A dribble of spit slid over his lips and he wiped it away. 'Just in case I ever come to a decision!'

I thought, oh hell, what have I uncovered here, because there was little doubt in my mind that 'just in case' did not enter the equation. He wasn't thinking over any decision. Stanley plus twelve finger-licking piranha adapted to live in Lake Taupo's coldest temperatures equalled hello rainbow trout, welcome to your new flatmates, courtesy of mad Stanley. Dunkie and I had always thought he had loopy tendencies.

Sitting there listening to his creaky harsh voice I felt my legs weaken with shock.

The skin on his face seemed to have tightened and he was glaring at me, challenging me to respond, because now I knew everything — he had wanted me to know — and he was waiting to hear what I would say. All I could think of were lines from 'Kubla Khan' (for the last time, as it happened):

> And 'mid the tumult Kubla heard from far
> Ancestral voices prophesying war!

Then he said, 'This place lacks something, Robbie! It lacks savagery!'

I hadn't a clue what to say. There didn't seem much point in starting a debate about whether the citizens of Taupo were the collection of avaricious ne'er-do-wells he imagined them to be. On that point his mind appeared to be well and truly made up. I felt like protesting that my Mum would be very annoyed if her fishing were to be ruined by a school of rampaging piranha. Stanley interpreted my glazed stare and lack of reaction as disbelief. 'Come with me,' he said, 'I'll show you!' He grabbed my wrist and hauled me to my feet. 'Come on!'

He strode away up the lawn towards the garage in that stiff-legged gait with his heels stomping into the ground, glancing behind to make sure that I was following.

He led me into the garage, squeezed round the end of the car, and went to the other side where a work-bench extended the length of the whole wall. Like work-benches in most garages, this one was cluttered with all manner of tools, boxes, tins and other odds and ends that had never been put away. A tiny cleared space in the middle watched and waited as the chaos closed in. Stanley crouched under the bench and beckoned me to come closer. He cleared away a pile of cardboard cartons and pointed. Underneath, among the cobwebs and dust, were four spanking-new chilly bins — ordinary chilly bins designed to carry picnics to the nearest beach on long hot summer days. I could tell they were new because they had a fresh plastic smell and the dust had not had a chance to infiltrate the old sheet that covered them.

Stanley looked at me triumphantly. 'There you are! Do you believe me now?'

I was perplexed, and it showed.

'Don't you understand?' he said. 'I've got them hidden away up here, all ready.'

'Four chilly bins. You've got four chilly bins ready for what?'

'To take them down to the lake. I'll put three of them in each one. Four different locations for release, you see? Or if I change my mind at the last minute and find an especially good spot, I can release six of them. It gives flexibility, that's the beauty of it.' He beamed at me, bright-eyed. 'Well? What do you think?'

I was thinking that I wanted to get out of that garage and out of that house and away from Stanley Swinton as fast as possible, and this time I knew that I wouldn't be returning. I tried to keep my face expressionless and turned to walk back round the car, muttering something about how interesting it all was — and then it happened.

I felt Stanley's hand fall on my shoulder, and I thought, oh hell, here we go again with the pleading bit and then he said, 'Robbie, don't go away, I don't want that to happen again.' I thought, he's really got it bad this time, and I tried to squirm and twist my shoulder away. It didn't work. His grip tightened. 'I don't care if you don't agree with me, but I want you to respect me. You must admire the way I've planned it. I'm not stupid, I'm not crazy and someone must know what I've done, and there's no one else.' I felt his other hand brush against my hair and his taut voice whispered, 'Celie, Celie,' and I thought, oh God, the screwball thinks I'm his daughter. Then his hand dropped in front of me. It was like watching something in slow motion as I saw his arm go round my waist. I leaned away from him, beginning to panic, and his hand slipped up against my breast and I thought, oh shit! I didn't know how to get away from him.

I could feel my face flushing but my hands were cold and sweaty. I tried to ease away from him. I said, 'Mr Swinton, I'm not Celie, I'm not your daughter.' But he would not release me. His arm tightened. His hand pressed against me. I couldn't see his face. I had no way of reading what he was thinking. If I had been able to see his face I think I could have handled it, but he was no longer Stanley — he had become a stranger behind me. There was an instant I recall so clearly, like a camera shutter flicking in my mind. I felt guilty! Can you imagine it? *Me* guilty! I saw faces questioning me. Then, from the past, I was standing in a church hall. The well-groomed lady in a track suit who was taking the self-defence course my mother had enrolled me in when I was at Intermediate was showing me how to knee a man in the groin, and she was saying, 'And remember, while you're doing it you must scream, "Nuts, nuts, nuts!" at the *top* of your voice.'

I think it was that absurdity that finally made me abandon control and cut loose. My arms flailed as I wrenched myself away and I felt my elbow jab into his stomach. I heard him scramble backwards. I crabbed and scrabbled around the front of the car, crashing my shins against the bumper, then looked over to the other side of the garage. One glance at Stanley cringing against the work-bench told me that this might be a nightmare of misunderstanding. His jaw was slack and he was muttering something like, 'I didn't mean anything, I thought you were her again.' I couldn't make out all the words.

I briefly felt frightened and remorseful once more, but then I thought, why in the hell should I? Damn him! He could take out his hang-ups over his dead bloody daughter on someone else! I'd never asked to look like her. And anyway, how was I to know what he really intended to do? Or wanted to do? He was trying to talk to me, but I refused to look at him again and I made for the door of the garage.

The house door was open and I ran straight inside into the kitchen. Elizabeth Amelia was fossicking in a cupboard and turned in astonishment as I hurtled in. 'Robbie! Whatever's the matter?'

I said the first thing that came into my head. 'I want a drink of water.'

She filled a glass, still watching me, and passed it across. 'You're trembling. Come through and sit down and tell me what's happened. Let me take the water.' She put an arm round my shoulder, led me to the sitting room and sat beside me on the sofa, her arm still around me. 'Now tell me!'

Hot tears suddenly spilled out of me, and the trembling stopped, pushed away by rage and fury that made me want to break things. 'I'll tell you! I'll tell you all right! That bloody husband of yours just tried to grope me, that's what's happened! Is that good enough for you?'

I stood up, feeling better every second. 'And I'll tell you something else the crazy old pervert is up to! He's going to put those homicidal bloody fish he keeps in the backyard into the lake! Did you know that? He's going to let them loose in the lake! How does that grab you, Elizabeth Amelia? How about that?'

She was rendered speechless, struck dumb and shattered with shock all at once. 'Dear God,' she muttered at last, 'dear God, dear God.'

My face glowed with satisfaction. 'Is that all you can say? What's the matter with you? Maybe you're as crazy as he is. Perhaps you're a bit kinky yourself. Are you?'

That one shafted home to a vital spot. She stood to face me. 'There's no need for that Robbie!'

'Up yours!' I said, but I could feel my rage draining away as fast as it had flooded through me. The tears came again, great sheets of them all over my cheeks as I stood there looking at her. Then I started sniffing and I didn't have a handkerchief. Elizabeth Amelia produced one out of her sleeve and said in a very quiet voice, 'Use this.'

She waited while I blew my nose and screwed the handkerchief around my eyes as though I were trying to scrape them clean. When she spoke her voice was very soft. 'Robbie, I am most dreadfully sorry. I had no idea. I should have been more watchful.' She looked directly at me. 'You had better stay away from here for the time being.'

'For the time being!' I muttered. 'Don't worry, you won't see me round here again.'

'I wouldn't blame you for that, but Robbie there are things you don't understand — about Stanley, I mean. There's something else I want to say — to ask of you.'

'Don't tell me,' I said. 'Keep it quiet, right? Hush it up? Don't tell anyone about Stanley and his friendly performing piranha? Fat chance!' I said bitterly. I felt like winding myself up into a rage again, but I didn't have the energy. 'How can you ask something like that? I mean, has this happened before? Does the old goat

114

make a habit of it? Are you going to keep on brushing Stanley under the carpet?'

She bit her lip, then to my utter amazement her eyes began to glisten. 'I haven't asked you to do anything yet have I? Wait here a moment.' She left the room. The house was so quiet I could hear her footsteps in the hall, the noise of a drawer opening at the far end of the house, then sliding shut. When she returned she held a blue aerogramme. 'Before you do anything I want you to read this.' She looked at me beseechingly. 'After that you can do what you like and I shall understand. But I would be most grateful if you would read this first, and later, if you're agreeable, I'd like to talk to you.'

I took it from her and glanced at the address. It was one of the envelopes she had dropped that day on the path, addressed to her personally at a Taupo Post Office box number. I don't know why I didn't open it there when she gave it to me. I stuffed it into my jeans pocket and said, 'I'll think about it.'

She accompanied me to the door. 'I'll phone you in a couple of days. Don't worry about the fish. I'll take care of them. I'm sorry. I blame myself. Please tell your parents to ring me if — if —'

I was sick of the sound of her voice. All I wanted to do was to get away from there. I smiled briefly and formally. There was no sign of Stanley. I'm not sure what I would have done if he had appeared. I pedalled away crouched over the handlebars, feeling the cleanness of the wind. I could recall the sensation of his fingers and I shook my head to blow it out of my hair.

When I reached home I walked inside feeling dazed and empty. My mother was standing at the sink. I went into the kitchen and stood beside her. She looked at me and put down the vegetable knife she had been using.

She lifted her arm behind me — then hesitated. I leaned against her and her arm enclosed me and hugged me. We stood together there for about a minute.

'I've finished working at the Swintons,' I said. 'We had an argument.'

'About what?'

'Nothing all that important. I'm all right, but I don't want to go back there. It's not the same anymore.'

She turned me so that I faced her. 'Robbie, you would tell me if there was something wrong, wouldn't you?'

I smiled and said, 'Of course I would. Where's Dad?'

'Where do you think?'

'Garage — right?'

'Where else?'

'I'll go and see what he's working on.'

I walked down the back path towards the garage from where I could hear the soft regular tapping of his hammer. I was going to tell him — about the fish anyway, and who knows what else — and to hell with Elizabeth Swinton and her whining. It was all too much to keep to myself. But before I reached him I felt the crinkle of paper in my pocket and pulled out the aerogramme as I was walking. I flipped it open and looked at the top, and my feet came to a sudden stop. It began, 'Dear Mum'. I looked at the last page. The letter itself was typed, but the paper had almost run out at the last line and the signature was handwritten in very small script at the bottom. But it was perfectly legible: 'Love from us all, Cecilia'.

Cecilia? Celie? The dead Cecilia? I returned the letter to my pocket and walked slowly back inside to my room. Elizabeth Amelia, I thought, your wish is granted.

XII
HISTORY

The return address was an apartment building somewhere in Sydney — something called Harbour View Towers. A quick perusal of the letter not only confirmed that Cecilia was alive and well, it also suggested that she was happily breeding in an Australian high rise and was thoroughly contented with her lot. At first I felt like screwing the thing into a tiny blue paper ball and tossing it into the waste bin. For months I had been led to believe that the Swinton offspring was languishing in paradise, and where was she? I suppose a cynic might say that, considering where she had turned up, she was enduring hell and serves her right, but this, on top of what the Swinton household had already dealt me that day, was a bit much! Why had Elizabeth Amelia led me to believe that Cecilia was dead?

Then I started to think. Putting aside the scenario of the Swinton parents being gnawed these long years by the death of their loved one, I began to piece together the new directions in the plot. I realized first that never once had I heard the words 'dead' or 'death' from either Stanley or his loving wife when speaking of their daughter. They had always referred to 'their loss' or Cecilia's 'departure', which I had assumed to be the standard euphemisms for death. But they had apparently meant every word they had said, in Stanley's case anyway. A reading of this letter left no doubt that Elizabeth Amelia herself had lost nothing of Cecilia except for the convenience of having her living in the next street, where she could visit the flourishing mob of grandchildren. It was a letter that reeked of glossy, domestic bliss.

Dear Mother,

It was good to receive your letter a couple of weeks ago. I'm sorry I haven't replied sooner, but we've been very busy with the finishing touches for the new apartment, and then of course there has been the whole business of moving in. We kept to the colour schemes we showed you when you were over here last year, and the whole effect is quite splendid. The decorator managed to get hold of some really marvellous fabric for the drapes in the master bedroom. I'm absolutely thrilled with it all.

Kevin has been away a lot lately supervising the last stages of the condominiums up in Brisbane. Most of them have been pre-leased now, but we are still keeping one in reserve, just in case. Mind you, I don't think Kevin will keep it aside for ever. You wouldn't believe the rents people are willing to pay up there these days.

Sharleen and Roddy have both ended up with good teachers this year and have loved going back to school. And do you realize that in a few months the twins will be off to school as well? God, they grow up fast don't they? They've both lost their front teeth which they think is great, because they're doing very well out of the tooth fairy at the moment. In fact I overheard Diana the other day chatting up one of her little friends and offering to take over any teeth that fall out and suggesting they split the proceeds. She takes after her father, that one. I've an undeveloped film in the camera with a few shots we took at the beach a couple of weeks ago and will send some photos in a week or two. The kids all send hugs and kisses and would love to see you when you manage to sneak away again.

Incidentally, when the twins finally get off to school, guess what I'm planning to do? I'm going to enrol for a couple of part-time courses at the university. A friend of mine is doing some papers towards a diploma in social services, and is really enjoying it, so I thought, why not? Better late than never, eh? I'm certainly not going to sit around the apartment all day playing bridge, and to hell with what dear Kevin says.

There was more of the same for a couple of paragraphs, then towards the end came this:

I'm glad your gardening girl is still working out well. What a shame about her friend. I still find it strange that the old man has taken to her so happily. In fact at times it worries me. I wonder what he is really seeing in her. I keep remembering how you said she looks so much as I did then. After what happened between the old boy and me, I should have thought that a second version would be the last thing he would want.

I folded the letter very carefully and let the clues about the new Cecilia begin to draw fresh outlines of her in my mind. But it refused to take shape. I could not picture her as someone who might have been produced by the kind of parents she had. Surely the pair of them must have passed along some trace of their personalities. Perhaps I was distracted by her comments in that paragraph towards the end.

Obviously her mother had kept Cecilia well informed about me, and the Swinton daughter had found me sufficiently interesting to turn me into a topic of conversation in her letters. It was equally obvious that Celie did not regard her father with reverence. Whatever had occurred between them in the past had not left her feeling in awe of him, nor it seemed with deep emotion of any kind. She spoke of him as if he were the family's pet spaniel, a shaggy smelly old beast whose occasional pranks could still raise eyebrows or provoke an indulgent smile.

This puzzled me. The Stanley I knew was not like that. Mind you, I wasn't sure of him anymore. I had thought I had more or less figured him out, but the revelations of that day when he had made a flanking attack on my bosom had left me a very wary young lady. You can perhaps detect from my choice of words that the shock of the experience did not scar me for life. In fact a day or two after it happened I was able to look back upon it with the faintest of smiles — the faintest of *grim* smiles. I recalled that this was the second time in a few months that someone had made a swoop for my boobs. But whereas Dunkie's lunge on the lake front had been the desperate act of an anxious youth despairing of ever reducing his state of innocence, Stanley's motives were another matter altogether, and there was no way I would ever look upon his little performance indulgently.

Yet, nasty and sinister as they might have been, his motives perplexed me, especially after I had read Cecilia's letter. Her words put a new light on her mother's plea that I should hesitate before exposing Stanley to the world as a kinky old slob, that there were things about him that I ought to know — exactly what Elizabeth Amelia had hoped would happen when she had given me the letter. So I hesitated and awaited the promised phone call.

Five days passed before it came. I know it was that many because I was counting them with mounting impatience. I was dying to know what was going on up there. I was almost on the point of ringing her myself when I was summoned to the phone on Saturday morning to hear Elizabeth Amelia's calm confident voice, as sweetly assured as it had ever been.

'Good morning my dear. I was wondering if you would care to join me for another of those morning teas we have become so accustomed to. I've made an enormous batch of scones, simply enormous.'

'All right then.'

'I'm so glad you feel able to come. We have such

a lot to talk about. You read my daughter's letter, I suppose?'

'Yes, I read it.'

'I imagined you had. I hope it didn't surprise you too much. I might have a few more surprises in store for you this morning. Shall we say in about an hour from now?'

'Yes, that'll be fine.'

'I'm so pleased. Incidentally, don't worry your head about Stanley. That matter is taken care of. I'll see you soon then.'

The matter of Stanley was taken care of! I couldn't help thinking of the vision of the family spaniel I had gleaned from the letter. I imagined him being dragged outside and chained to his kennel for a week as punishment for doing whoopsies on the carpet.

Despite the implacable confidence of Elizabeth Amelia's voice, I approached the Swinton house with trepidation. I thought I had put my feelings into perspective, but as I rode up the hill I knew that I dreaded confronting Stanley again. If he had been anywhere in sight I think I would have instantly turned and pedalled away. But he was nowhere to be seen. The garage was open. The car wasn't there and I was interested to see that someone had been clearing away the accumulated junk of many years. The work-bench was completely bare and there was nothing whatever underneath. The cardboard cartons and the bright new chilly bins had disappeared.

Elizabeth Amelia must have been looking out for me because she appeared on the front step as soon as I had leaned my bicycle against the side of the house. 'Good morning, Robbie,' she said, 'do come in.' I smiled and followed her inside. 'I know I keep saying it, but I really am so grateful that you came — that you waited.'

'It's quite OK,' I said.

'It is not OK. I have been worrying myself sick about what happened. I will never forgive myself. But at least it told me what had to be done. Come along, I have the coffee ready through here.'

She led me to the sitting room, which was far from its usual self. There was no sign of the spinning-wheel, and the small paintings and prints had all been removed from the panelled wall. Most of the books had been piled in small stacks on the shelves. Altogether, unmistakable signs of someone doing some half-hearted packing.

'What's happening?' I asked. 'You look as though you're getting ready to move.'

'We'll get to that later,' she said. 'We have a lot to talk about first.' She poured coffee and passed me the scones. 'Did you bring Cecilia's letter?' I passed it over. 'Did it surprise you? I rather thought it would. As you might have guessed, that was my intention.'

'Of course it surprised me,' I said. 'I mean, you had as good as told me more than once that she was dead.'

'As good as, yes, but not quite.' She smiled contentedly. 'I always stopped just short of using that dreadful final word didn't I? And you thought it was because I couldn't bring myself to pronounce it. Well, no matter, you are fully aware now that Celie is alive and well and leading a happy life in Sydney.'

I nodded. 'That's plain enough. What I can't understand is why you had to pretend. What's the reason for all the — all the —'

'Fantasy?'

'That wasn't the word I had in mind, but it'll do.'

'It was all to do with Stanley, and still is, I suppose. If Stanley hadn't made such an ass of himself with you the other day, I imagine it would have drifted on forever. But then again, if Stanley hadn't disgraced himself his devious little plot with the beastly fish would

122

never have come to light.'

'I'm so glad I was able to help,' I said tartly. 'You must have known what he was up to with the fish. You knew they were there and what they were. Dunkie and I saw you feeding them. I talked to you about them.'

'Naturally I knew about them,' she snapped, 'but believe me, I was not aware of Stanley's intentions.'

'Why not? You know those fish are dangerous.'

'*Were* dangerous.'

'What's happened to them?'

'They have been disposed of. They are dead. They are buried in one of Stanley's herb gardens, about one metre under. The herbs in question are also dead.'

I munched on a scone and regarded her thoughtfully. An unfamiliar bite had edged into Mrs Swinton's voice, a flinty hardness that had never been there before. I realized that I was even thinking of her as Mrs Swinton, rather than the friendly, patient Elizabeth Amelia.

'How did you kill them?'

'We poured disinfectant into the tanks. It proved very effective.'

I'll bet it did, I thought, and very sanitizing with it. Then I pounced on the pronoun, which had not escaped my vigilance. 'You said "we" poured it in. Do you mean Stanley actually helped you?'

'Dear me, no. Stanley was lying around somewhere grieving at the time. No, Cecilia helped me.'

'Cecilia? Is she here?'

'She is.' I looked around the room. 'But not in the house at the moment. She's down in the town at the bank helping Stanley to sign some documents. They'll be back before long, and you'll meet her then.'

'I'm not sure that I want to — '

'Meet Cecilia?'

'No, Mr Swinton. I'm not sure — '

'You don't have to see Stanley again if you'd rather not, though I think you'd notice a few changes in him. He really is most contrite and ashamed of himself — a changed man.'

I had a growing impression that the knives were out for Stanley. Something had definitely happened to his quaint little wife that had little to do with loving, honouring, and obeying. She wasn't missing the smallest chance to shred him.

'How long has Cecilia been here?'

'She flew over at once after I phoned last Monday.'

'I still can't imagine how Mr Swinton let you kill his fish after all he'd done to get them here.'

'He had little choice in the matter. What, incidentally, do you know about how he brought those fish here? What has Stanley said to you? That's what I'd really like to talk about.'

So I launched into the tales Stanley had told me, together with all I had imagined and surmised. As I talked, another change came over Elizabeth Amelia and her eyes filled up with sadness as though my words were raking up memories and emotions that had been tucked safely away for a long, long time.

When I had finished she muttered, 'What a mess, what a mess. Poor Stanley. The silly deluded man. Now it has come to this. The silly, silly man.'

All of which was quite unlike her usual confident pronouncements. Perhaps she was missing her spinning-wheel. This was the first time I had ever talked to her at length without the whirring wheel driving along as an accompaniment to her voice.

She sat back in the chair with her head resting on the cushion and said, 'Now I'll tell you the real story of Stanley. I'll start with the fish. Stanley's piranha.' She fidgeted, trying to get herself comfortable. 'The trouble is, there are so many places where I could begin, it's 'hard to know what to say first.'

'The piranha?' I prompted. 'Where did they come from?'

'Well, they didn't come from backwater bayous in the Amazon,' she said. 'Stanley has never been near the head-waters of the Amazon in his life. The piranha came originally from some disreputable pet shop dealer in Los Angeles who used to specialize in distributing his more bizarre specimens around the world through seamen in cargo ships who wanted to earn a few extra dollars.'

All that came out in one breath. Elizabeth Amelia certainly knew how to open with a show-stopper! I was actually conscious of my jaw dropping open. 'He what?'

'He found a classified advertisement in one of those cheap true life adventure magazines. I don't know whether they're around anymore, but in those days they were quite popular. Anyway, he noticed this advertisement from someone in Los Angeles, giving a box number. He underlined it heavily and I happened to see it. I can still remember the words. "How would you like to see some living danger in your own home? Send now for a free brochure to — " whatever the box number was.

'Then a couple of cyclostyled sheets of paper turned up in an envelope with a US postage stamp, and I managed to get a peek at those too. The entrepreneur called himself Rodriguez and he specialized in catering for exotic tastes in pets. If you wanted a scorpion, a tarantula, or a rattlesnake to play with in the privacy of your own home, Senor Rodriguez could help. All the tantalizing dangers you've ever read about coming your way by post, and overseas customers could be catered for through a special shipping service. That was about all I managed to see, but it was enough. So when I noticed Stanley a couple of months later paying a lot of attention to the shipping news in the newspaper, it didn't take much deduction to work out what was going on. Stanley has an unfortunate habit of leaving obvious tracks. He has a passion for underlining things that attract his attention, or that he wants to remember. One morning I noticed that he had underlined the arrival date in Auckland of a freighter outward bound from California via Honolulu and Suva.

'I waited. Sure enough, on the day the ship was due to arrive, Stanley suddenly found that he had to make a trip to Auckland. The following day he came back with an enormous vacuum flask, and I pounced!

'With a very innocent face he showed me a few harmless looking baby fish, which he assured me were nothing more than some specimens of a rare tropical species which were to be the nucleus of an aquarium. What could I say? I was certain that the way he'd got hold of them was illegal. They must have been brought in by some co-operative crew member, presumably for a fee, but I could not really see any genuine harm in what had happened. To tell you the truth, I was mentally prepared for a cobra or a rattlesnake or something, and to see a few tiny fish was a relief! Besides, Stanley seemed to be utterly captivated by them, and at that time there was nothing more I wanted in this world than to have Stanley absorbed in something — completely absorbed.'

'But you must have found out very quickly what they really were.'

'Eventually I did, but by that time I couldn't see anything to worry about. So Stanley's hobby was rearing piranha? What did it matter? By the time I discovered what those fish really were they had become part of the place. They were Stanley's little hobby, and I could think of many things much worse that Stanley could have taken up as a private interest.'

'But why did all this happen? Why on earth did he want to own those things in the first place?'

'The answer to that takes us into deeper water,' said Elizabeth Amelia. She had become more expansive as she talked, more assured like someone whose memory was reviving, a Viking story-teller who finds the words of a saga coming back. 'The fish arrived soon after Stanley filled in the swimming pool and landscaped the lawn and what was once the vegetable garden. Then he began planting trees. All that happened when Cecilia left home.'

I needed to establish a few simple facts. 'Has Stanley ever been to South America? Has he ever lived there?'

'It depends on what you mean by lived. Actually lived there? No. But inside him, in his spirit, I doubt if he's ever really lived anywhere else.'

'But he's never actually been there?'

'He paid a fleeting visit when he was a boy, but it was long enough for him to catch two bugs. One of them was smallpox. The other was an obsession with some half-real place that has grown in his mind ever since. You see, Stanley came to New Zealand when he was a boy, with his parents. They were immigrants. In those days the ships from what we used to call the Home Country took their time getting here, and Stanley's family travelled on a freighter that made a port of call at some place in the lower reaches of the Amazon. He was hooked from the moment someone slung a bucket over the side two hundred kilometres from the coast and hauled it up full of fresh water. That's what the force of the water flowing from the Amazon's mouth can do. It can push its way like a tongue into the ocean for more than two hundred kilometres before it becomes salty.

'Then the ship sailed up the lower stretches of the river and Stanley, standing on the deck, saw the

Amazon rain forest in the distance for the first and only time. You must remember that this was more than fifty years ago. Things couldn't have changed all that much from the times when the explorers in pith helmets set off up river in canoes. Anyway, Stanley was apparently smitten by the Amazon, just before he was bitten by the smallpox. He recovered from the disease, which was a small miracle, with his body scarred and pitted for life, but he didn't recover from the Amazon.'

'Did you find all this about Mr Swinton when you married him?' I asked.

'Oh no, I've known about most of it from the time his family moved in next door to us in Wellington. You see Stanley and I have known each other from the time we were in primary school together.'

'Why did you marry him?'

She laughed. 'Why on earth do you think? Because I loved him.'

'I'm sorry, I didn't intend it to sound like that.'

'People change, Robbie,' she said. 'When Stanley was a young man he had a vision, and he wanted me to be a part of it. He was very lonely, even then. The disease had left his face scarred. You mightn't think it to look at him now, but as a young man he was very pale and gaunt — it was only later that he worked on his sun-tan. People tended to shuffle away from him. He had a very hard time at school. Children can be very cruel, as I suppose you know, and that made him worse. They used to call him Poxy Swinton. Do you know what someone did when he was in the sixth form? Someone cut out his face from the photograph of school librarians in the previous year's school magazine. This person pasted it on a piece of paper and wrote underneath, "Do you suffer from acne? Just think how worse off you could be! Take a look at this!" This person then pinned it to the notice-board in Stanley's form room. When his form teacher saw it, he laughed. So when the real world became too much he began to dream, and then I suppose he began to live in his dream.'

'He dreamed about the Amazon. You said that he had a vision.'

'He had a vision. It changed from time to time. Sometimes we were going to be missionaries living in a thatched bungalow in a jungle clearing, dispensing medicine and comfort to the sick — the Albert Schweitzers of the Amazon. Sometimes we were going to be planters living in a magnificent mansion among our acres won from the jungle. At other times I could see him looking inside himself at goodness knows what strange dream. Anyway, I married him because of all that. Other young women married men because they had good, steady jobs and bright prospects for the future. I married Stanley because he was a dreamer.'

I heard a car pulling up outside and I shifted in my chair.

'Don't worry,' said Elizabeth Amelia. 'Stanley will not bother you. Cecilia is here.'

'What happened?'

'To what?'

'The visions. The dreams. What happened to them? You never went to South America did you?'

'No, we never went anywhere, unless you call moving round half a dozen towns and cities in New Zealand going somewhere. You see, Stanley was not what you would call a success in life.'

A voice came from the door — clear, precise, and hard. 'In fact Stanley was a bit of a failure, wasn't he, Mother? How do you do, you must be Robbie. I'm Cecilia.'

XIII
CECILIA

At first I could have sworn it was Stanley I heard, but when I turned I saw the face Elizabeth Amelia had shown me in that photograph several months before. It had grown older and firmer. The heavy eyebrows had gone, plucked into two neat half moons with razor sharp edges. They made her tilted nose look more pugnacious, and I noticed that she had inherited Stanley's mouth, with the same lips that seemed to flex when they moved. Her hair was still shoulder length, but combed very straight with a carefully cut fringe sweeping across her forehead. Her clothes were carefully casual — faded jeans and pastel sneakers with a shirt to match and, just to show she could afford anything she wanted, a soft leather jerkin.

She flopped down in an armchair and beamed at us. 'I suppose Mother has been bringing you up to date on the events of the past couple of days. Have you, Mother?'

'I haven't really had the time, dear.'

'We *are* back rather early,' said Cecilia. 'The bank wasn't open. I wish you'd told me.'

'I completely forgot it was a Saturday.'

'Never mind, we can fix up the transfer of funds on Monday morning. I'll have time.' She turned to me. 'So you're the Robbie Mother has told me so much about. Did I really look like that when I was your age? I suppose I did. It's so hard to remember. I suppose Mother has at least told you the news, has she?'

'I'm not sure what you mean,' I said quietly. I was still trying to adjust to Cecilia. Her letter had told me that she was not the shy, retiring kind, but seeing her in the flesh she reminded me of a sleek, efficient barracuda who has been to charm school. She was no piranha. She would bite when it suited her, not just when she smelt blood. She was menacing. I disliked her as soon as she opened her mouth.

She raised her eyebrows. 'So Mother hasn't told you she'll be moving?'

'No. Moving where to?'

'To Brisbane. My husband has almost completed a new apartment development in Surfers' Paradise and one of the apartments is reserved for Mother, isn't it Mother? She's always wanted to join us in Australia, haven't you, Mother?'

Mother said nothing.

'What about Mr Swinton?' I asked.

'Father? Oh yes, he'll be coming too. We could hardly leave him behind, could we? Especially after what he's been up to. Lord knows how he'd behave if we left him here unattended. Which reminds me. . . '

She rose elegantly and paced to the doorway. 'Father! Come through here a moment will you?' I heard a voice at the other end of the house. Cecilia disappeared up the hall and we could hear muffled voices arguing. I looked at Elizabeth Amelia in time to see her turn quickly away. She had been staring at me. I could tell she had been trying to gauge my reaction to her daughter. She refused to catch my eye and I could see her mouth tightening. She knew what I was thinking. I was thinking, 'Of all the people your daughter could have been, I would never have picked this one.' I wondered if her mouth had tightened through determination, or shame and embarrassment.

We did not speak while Cecilia was out of the room. When she returned she was leading Stanley. He walked slowly, his eyes narrowed to slits and his mouth creased on his face. But she led him by some invisible cord he could not resist. Cecilia was grinning. 'Here's

Father!' she said brightly. 'I've persuaded him to come and apologize to you Robbie for his silly behaviour the other day. None of us can imagine what came over him, can we, Mother?'

Elizabeth Amelia smiled and looked at me uncertainly. 'He really is sorry, Robbie.'

'Of course he is,' breezed Cecilia. 'Now you go and sit down over there, Father. I'm so glad we've got that out of the way! Oh, is that coffee? And scones? I haven't tasted home-made scones for years.'

She bustled about pouring coffee for herself and refilling her mother's cup. Stanley had walked slowly to the far side of the room and was sitting on a low divan. It didn't match his size and he looked awkward and uncomfortable. While Cecilia chattered, his head turned slowly and met my gaze. He did not look away when he saw that I was watching him. He stared back. His lips quivered and he only turned away when he began to blink rapidly. No one else noticed.

Meanwhile Cecilia had equipped herself with coffee and scones and was seated ever-so-elegantly on a high-backed chair. 'Just think,' she said, 'by this time next week you'll be settled in your new home.'

'Why are you going?' I asked Elizabeth Amelia.

'Because we think it's time for the family to be closer together again,' said Cecilia.

Her mother hesitated, then to my relief spoke directly to me. 'We're going because there is not really much choice,' she said, 'and it won't be very different from living here.'

'What Mother means,' said Cecilia, 'is that she has nothing to hold her here anymore. If it comes to that, there was never much keeping her here in the first place, but now that Kevin's investments have started to bring in the money, it makes sense to be there to enjoy it all.' I looked at her blankly. She wiped a crumb from the corner of her mouth and continued, 'It's really neither here nor there as far as you're concerned, but Mother is the financial support of my parents, aren't you, Mother? You must have wondered why Father stayed around the house all day playing in his garden. It's simply because of Mother's investments.'

Elizabeth Amelia butted in. 'What Cecilia is saying, Robbie, is that we live on the income from an inheritance I received when my parents died. They owned a block of land north of Wellington in the hills which turned out to be rather valuable when a property developer decided to build a suburb on it. When Cecilia married I gave most of it to her husband to help get him started, on the understanding that we share the profits from whatever he did with it, and now —'

'And now he's made his first million or so,' said Cecilia. 'The profits are pouring in, and it's time for Mother to start enjoying herself, isn't it Mother?'

'Why can't she enjoy the profits here?' I asked.

'I beg your pardon?'

'I said, why can't she enjoy the profits here?'

Cecilia regarded me very coolly indeed. 'Because it's not convenient. You wouldn't understand the complexities of transferring funds and all that sort of thing.'

'It's not difficult,' I said. 'All you have to do is arrange for a regular banker's draft.'

'I dare say,' said Cecilia, brushing imaginary crumbs from her lap, 'but there are other things involved as well.'

'It's because of him, isn't it?'

'Him?'

'Yes, him. Him sitting over there in the corner. The man behind you. Him on the divan. Your father!'

'Don't you think you're becoming a trifle impertinent?'

133

'You hate him don't you?'

'I beg your pardon?' She glared at me, trying to give me a withering shot of the evils, but she wasn't very good at it. She needed to take lessons from a teacher.

'Why do you hate him? Why do you hate your father?'

'I don't hate my father!' she blustered. 'And even if I did, I can't see why you should be concerned after what he did to you!'

'You don't care about what he did to me.'

'What an absurd thing to say! Of course I care! How could you say such a thing?'

'You just want him out of the way. Get him under cover where you can keep an eye on him.'

I shot a quick glance at Elizabeth Amelia to see how she was taking all this. To my surprise she seemed to be enjoying it immensely. So why, I thought, haven't you done this yourself long ago?

Cecilia, meanwhile, had made an effort to gather together the fragments of her shattered poise and had leaned back, casually looping an arm over one corner of the back of the chair. 'Let me assure you, young lady, that I haven't the faintest interest in keeping an eye on my father, as you put it. All I desire is that my parents should be happy in their old age. Furthermore, I'm beginning to find you rather tiresome and rude and —'

'Do you remember rubbing his tooth?'

'I beg your pardon.'

'Why do you keep saying that when you've heard me perfectly well?' I'd decided, what the hell, let's throw proverbial caution to the winds and see what happens. The result was most satisfying. Cecilia's cheeks turned red, quite overpowering the rouge, and I thought for a moment that she was going to stand up and head in my direction. But she managed to control herself. I

134

probed again. 'Do you remember polishing his golden tooth, polishing it until it gleamed?'

She breathed deeply and looked at me for the first time with some kind of understanding. 'Yes,' she said calmly, 'I remember polishing the golden tooth. I had a special piece of soft cloth which I kept on my dressing-table, and I used to sit on his knee every night and polish the fabulous golden tooth, and I used to ask him when I could have a golden tooth too. He would rub his fingers through my hair and say, "Celie, one day you will have as many golden teeth as you want, you wait and see." So does that answer your question to your satisfaction — Miss Kemp, isn't it?'

I kept quiet. She was still staring at me. The room had grown very silent and I could hear the air whistling from her nostrils. She reminded me of Stanley. Her whole mood now reminded me of Stanley. I waited.

'Shall I tell you some more, Miss Kemp?' Her voice bit viciously on my name. 'Would you like to hear some more?'

'Celie, I think we've heard quite enough.' Elizabeth Amelia reached and put her hand on her daughter's arm, but she twisted away.

'No Mother, I'm in the mood for talking. I want to talk to Miss Kemp, because I think I owe it to her to tell her what she so obviously wants to know, even if she hasn't got round to asking yet. She doesn't seem to like beg-your-pardons, so we'll have no more of them. We'll have no more polite phrases, just a few truths from the home front.

'The question is, which home do we start with? Not this one, because this was the one that came with Mother's money. This was the house we finally bought after Father gave in and we stopped trekking from one run-down house-hovel-bach to another. Note that I didn't use the words "apartment" or "flat". Father always drew the line at that. He always insisted on a section, a bit of land where we could breathe, as he so elegantly put it. Never mind that what you breathed in might be the neighbour's drains just over the fence. "A bit of land," he always used to say, "it's important to have a bit of land!" Dear God, some of the bits of land we lived on would have made a gravel pit seem like paradise.

'When we moved to a new place I always knew when we were nearing the new home. When the car began to drive down poky streets with all the houses the same, or when the tar-seal stopped and the pot-holes started, or when the roofing iron was painted with rust, I knew we were nearly at another home and another bloody school and another bunch of strange kids asking me why I talked so posh. Did I think I was stuck-up or something? Hey kids! We've found another victim called Cecilia. Ce-cil-ia, Ce-cil-ia, won't you let me feeeel-ya! Oh, I had such a jolly, ripping childhood, Robbie dear. It was an unforgettable experience, and I owe every delightful minute of it to my father, don't I, Father?'

All three of us turned to the corner, to discover that it was empty. Stanley had quietly slipped away and I, at least, had been so engrossed in Cecilia's memories that I had not noticed him go. He must have departed through the front door.

'Never mind,' said Cecilia, 'he knows the story anyway.'

'We weren't that badly off, Celie,' said her mother. 'We never lacked for a roof. There were many worse off than we were.'

'Oh I know, I know!' Cecilia snapped. 'I'm not complaining about the way we lived or even the moving round — '

'Why did you move around so much?' I said.

'Because Father was a salesman who wasn't very good at selling, and every time he was found out we had to leave the district — those things have a way of getting round prospective employers. No one wants to hire a door-to-door salesman who is a bit of a joke. And his daughter learns to cringe when the kids get to know who the oddball is who called at their house the other day, because his daughter knows they will tell her about it, every nauseating detail of the funny man dressed in a suit who talked as though he was lord of the manor deigning to do business with the peasants. She knows too that the time will soon arrive when the furniture van will be pulling up at the door to take the Swintons' belongings somewhere else. Once the kids know about your old man, you can be damned sure everyone else does too.'

'What did he sell?'

'Anything — cosmetics, brushes, fire extinguishers, furniture polish, insurance — you name it and Stanley's had a go at selling it. And through all those years I sat on his knee and he filled me with tales about this marvellous El Dorado, the enchanted forests which he had visited when young, and how we were going to live there in the shady glades, and so on, and so on! I don't want to go over all that again. Let's forget it!'

'Did you laugh at him?' I asked.

'Laugh at him?'

'Yes, did you ever laugh at him? Make fun of him?'

'Why do you ask that?'

'Because he thought I was laughing at him once, and I thought he was going to hit me.'

'Yes, I laughed at him once. No, let's get this right. I laughed at him once out loud. Then I shrieked at him. Before that I'd laughed at him to myself, so many times I'd lost count. Smiles and chuckles and laughs that I kept to myself. Then I laughed at him straight to his face. Then I packed a suitcase and left.' Her face was quivering, the memories stirring like the points of sharp pins.

'What did you say when you shrieked at him?'

'I don't remember exactly. All I recall is the exquisite pleasure in screaming at him.'

Elizabeth Amelia spoke up quietly. I had almost forgotten that she was there. 'You called him a pompous old fraud, dear. Then you said he was a useless phoney.'

'Yes, I did didn't I?' said Cecilia. 'Then I tried to scratch his face, and I told him I was going to give him a few more scars to remember me by.' She spoke slowly and reflectively and I could tell that she recalled every second of what must have been a memorable scene. 'Mind you, Robbie,' she continued, 'you must realize that in that little episode I let fly with everything I had never said in the years before. It was what you might call a jam-packed moment in time, and it blew up with quite a bang, didn't it Mother?'

I was dying to know what had set off the big bang and sent the Swinton universe spinning in unexpected directions. I didn't have to ask. Cecilia twisted a handkerchief slowly round a finger and became almost nostalgic. 'He just wouldn't let me grow up, would he? He wouldn't let me leave fantasy land. That endless droning voice telling me all about what we were going to do and what we were going to be. I let him give me wildlife picture books every birthday, and I even managed to look pleased when he gave me a paperback reprint of *The Origin of Species* for Christmas when I was fifteen. They all worked their way into the big cupboard in the hall, and yesterday morning they all went to the dump — every last one of them.

'And I bit my tongue and held my peace when he used to collect me from socials and parties by walking into the hall or into the house, right up to where I was,

138

and say, "Come along now Cecilia, it's time we were going."'

I cringed at the very thought. The adolescent Celie had undoubtedly suffered the occasional sling and arrow.

'Mind you,' she said, 'I didn't have to cope with too many invitations to parties — or anything for that matter — especially if it was a boy doing the inviting. After he'd interviewed the first two in the living-room as to their backgrounds and personal qualities, the applications to escort me anywhere quickly declined. Then he had the nerve to ask me why I never seemed to go out. "What's this Celie? Sitting at home on a nice afternoon like this? Why, I remember at your age — etc., etc!"

'But the biggie came when I was in the sixth form doing U.E. Geography. You don't have University Entrance anymore, do you? You call it something else — never mind. We were studying South America. Somehow our teacher bumped into Father, who must have reminisced about his imaginary sojourns in the Amazon, the Mato Grosso and all points north, east, and west. One morning Father smiled smugly as I left for school and announced in an oh-so-mysterious voice that I might be seeing him again sooner than I expected.

'How right he was. We had geography that morning in period two. I recall every detail. The teacher was a few minutes late. When he walked in he was accompanying Father. Father, it transpired, had spent many years living in the very area we were studying at the moment, and Father had kindly offered to come along and talk to the class on the topic, "My Life in the Jungle". Wasn't that nice of him! He would be able to give a new slant on the whole subject, a fresh perspective that would be most rewarding! At this point my class-mates shot a few puzzled glances in my direction. I barely noticed them because I knew what was going to happen.

'You see, Father was most unlucky. If he had told me about his little talk, I would have given him a very important item of information. Our geography teacher was new to the school. He had not long returned from working on a development project in Brazil under the auspices of some missionary group. The project was to do with surveying the food resources of the Amazon Basin. It had involved our teacher doing a lot of travelling. He had told us all about it. Then Father gave us the Swinton version.'

There was a long pause. Cecilia was reliving every minute of that geography period. 'I suppose it was embarrassing,' I said tentatively.

Cecilia gazed ruefully at me, as though she had learned to adjust to the memory. 'It was the most humiliating experience of my life. When I reached home that day, Father was waiting for me. He was *most* annoyed. Why had everyone smiled at him? He thought it was most ill-mannered of them. Even the teacher seemed amused! And as for me, what did I mean by hurrying out of the room at the end of the period and not waiting to talk to him? That was when I blew up,' she said, shrugging her shoulders.

'So now Robbie, you know most of what there is to know, and I really couldn't care less what you think. I don't *hate* my father. I suppose you could say I'm numb. My adolescence was like having a long-lasting anaesthetic slowly drip-fed into me. That's what it felt like anyway, and there's nothing much I can do about it now — there's nothing I *want* to do about it now. In fact, all I want to do now is to get on with the packing and organizing so we can ship out of here and leave it all behind. As far as I'm concerned, it was all over long ago.'

When she had left the room I said to Elizabeth Amelia, 'I didn't know that Cecilia went to school here.'

'Cecilia was never the kind of child who appears in old photographs on school walls,' she said.

'Was all that true?'

She sighed. 'Yes, it was all true for Cecilia, but if you asked Stanley he would tell you differently.'

'It wasn't all over for him was it?'

'No, I'm afraid it wasn't. What happened to you showed us that didn't it?'

'But couldn't you have done something? I mean, if you saw what was going on. . . .'

She looked at me sharply. 'Don't think for a moment that I was oblivious to what was happening. Give me credit for some sense. But what was I to do? Who was I supposed to choose? My husband or my daughter? You see, I would have had to take sides. So I did nothing much, just tried to smooth over the differences hoping that time would work things out. Well, now it has. Stanley and I are off to live in retirement in Surfers' Paradise. Wouldn't you say that's a nice happy ending?'

The question is, I thought, does Stanley think it is a nice happy ending? My last glimpse of him had reminded me of something from Mount Olympus bottling up a whole barrelful of wrath. 'Do you mind if I go down and have a last look at the garden? I won't be up here again, I guess, unless the new owners want someone to mow the lawns.'

'Of course, my dear,' said Elizabeth Amelia with one of her old, warm smiles. 'You'll see a few changes. The land agent suggested to Cecilia that the presentation of the property needed to be altered if we wanted to make a quick sale. Put your head round the door on the way out and say goodbye.'

If I knew my Stanley, things would not be over to

his satisfaction until he had carried out one final task. I knew I would find him somewhere in the garden. When I walked through the garage I found Cecilia piling some odds and ends into boxes. 'I'm having a last look at the garden,' I said.

'You'll notice one or two changes,' she responded grimly.

That was two warnings. When I reached the top of the lawn I could see what they meant. All the big trees down at the back had been topped, revealing the red brick wall and tiled roof of the house at the back. Walking nearer I could see that the ferns that had grown under the shelter of the canopies had been crushed and flattened. I strolled round the bottom loop path, picking my way through twigs and branches, and walked back up towards the aquarium. The door swung open and at a glance I could see that the building was bare. The tanks were piled untidily on the lawn outside.

Then I saw Stanley. He was beside one of the shrub beds, now nothing but freshly dug earth. His hands were buried in his pockets and he was standing with one foot resting on the border, just looking. He had seen me but he kept his eyes averted. Did I want to walk over and make friends? No, not really. I had no intention of restoring any sense of trust or understanding.

But I went closer. 'Someone's been busy,' I said, nodding my head to the decapitated trees.

His voice was low and thick. 'They got to them from next door. They'll be finishing the job in a couple of days.' He kept his eyes on the earth at his feet.

'Is that where they're buried?'

'They dug a deep pit and emptied the tanks in here. It'll grow a nice patch of lawn one day.'

He was looking at me now. His face was sullen, but his eyes were different. They did not have the matching look of defeat. I had seen loss and despair in the eyes of others, but here I was seeing something that was more like defiance.

'They put them all in there, did they?' I asked casually.

I could tell that he was choosing his words carefully. 'All the fish they poisoned are in there,' he said. 'Every last one of them.'

I wanted to know more, but I knew he would evade my questions so I simply said, 'I have to go now.' He did not reply. I tried again. 'Good luck'.

He raised his hand in a half-hearted wave and turned back to contemplate the remains of his forest. When I was part way up the lawn I glanced back. I was in time to see him watching me before he quickly turned away.

I walked through the garage. Cecilia was still there packing up tools and old tins of paint, with her mother helping her now. 'Well Robbie, I suppose we must say goodbye,' said Elizabeth Amelia. 'Such a pity we have to part in this way.'

'It's all happened rather suddenly, hasn't it?' I said. 'I suppose I'd better let you get on with your work.' I smiled and started to move off, then added, 'What did you do with the chilly bins?'

'What chilly bins?'

'The ones under the work-bench.'

'I didn't see anything like that under the work-bench. Did you Cecilia?'

Cecilia looked up from a scattering of rusty nails and bolts that she was sweeping up. 'Chilly bins? No, I haven't come across anything like that. Why do you ask?'

'Oh, nothing,' I said, shrugging it off. 'I must have been mistaken.'

XIV
MEMENTOES

I rode away from the Swintons that day greatly relieved at having parted company from that strange triangle. A few months earlier I would never have thought that I would think of my own home as a sanctuary of security and normality, but that day I was glad to walk back into it.

I never saw the Swintons again, nor heard anything from them, but I thought about them often, especially Stanley. I imagined him sitting in a smartly furnished apartment near the sea, lonely and bitter, brooding about what he had left behind. But brooding regretfully or with anticipation? Was he growing old and looking forward to death? I couldn't imagine Cecilia and her flock bringing him much joy and solace. Or was he quietly preserving every muscle and cell for as long as possible, waiting for news like an old prophet whose dearest wish is to be able to say, 'Vengeance is mine!'

I completed my seventh form year with much credit to myself, to the astonishment of some of my teachers who lacked the perception to see yet another transformation in me, as I quietly studied without making it too obvious. When March came the following year, it was I who went to university. Going to university in March became a kind of anniversary for me, and I knew it always would be, even after I had left the lecture rooms far behind me, and other memories of my youth faded. I even found my memories of Stanley beginning to blur, transforming him into a harmless old eccentric with daughter troubles.

But at the end of my second year at university I came home for the long vacation, and two things happened on one day which brought every detail of those months among the Swintons back into my mind.

I had never been near the Swintons' old house since their departure. One morning I went for a long walk and decided on an impulse to stroll up the hill where I had ridden so many times before, just out of curiosity. The outside of the front of the house looked the same. Different curtains hung at the windows and the roof was a new colour, but nothing had really changed. I stopped at the gate. Everything seemed to be shut up, the owners presumably working or shopping with their children safely at school. The garage door was closed.

I wanted to have a quick peek around the back. If anyone questioned me I could always say I was a Mormon missionary or something, looking for the front door and a possible convert. I walked quickly round the side of the house that faced the lake and moved down to the back lawn. The mown grass stretched on all sides to the fences, which were made of vertical palings painted alternately in red and white. A clothes-line revolved slowly in the breeze. A barbecue made of concrete blocks had replaced the aquarium. The peas in the vegetable garden were coming into flower and the plastic compost tub in one corner was overflowing with weeds and lawn clippings.

'Can I help you?'

I spun round to see a smiling, fresh-faced woman standing behind me carrying a laden clothes-basket. She didn't seem at all outraged to find me standing on her back lawn, and I thankfully abandoned my missionary ploy. 'I'm sorry I came round the back without knocking first. I didn't realize anyone was at home.'

'That's all right,' she said, waiting.

'This might seem strange,' I said, 'but I wanted to look at the back of the section. I once worked for the previous owner. He had a very big garden and I wanted to see what it looked like now.'

'So you worked in Mr Swinton's garden,' she said, 'or perhaps I should say jungle, from what I've heard from the neighbours. If what they say is true, it must have been quite a sight!' Her voice made it perfectly clear that she was not referring to a sight to be admired. 'It had virtually gone when we moved in,' she said, 'apart from a few shrubs. In fact the whole place looked a bit of a mess. He must have had an enormous number of trees.'

I nodded. 'There were plenty of trees.'

'Well, as you can see, we put the whole back of the section into lawn. It's much safer for the children when they want to play.' She looked at me sharply. 'Now, wait a minute, you're just the person who might be able to solve something that's been puzzling us.'

'If I can,' I said.

She led me further down the lawn and pointed. 'Do you see that patch of grass? The spot over towards the fence? It must have been an old flower bed, but we've never understood why the lawn on that patch has grown so vigorously, and so much greener than the rest. Can you see what I mean?'

I could indeed. It was a truly aristocratic circle of lawn that would have made any greenkeeper feel proud. 'I think it was a herb bed,' I said. 'I seem to remember Mr Swinton dumping a load of manure in it to give it a boost.'

'It certainly worked,' said the woman of the house. (So did the disinfectant, lady!)

We chatted for a few minutes, then I made my farewells with many thanks for her letting me stroll around her property uninvited. I had planned to go down to the town for a pre-Christmas survey of the shops, but when I began walking along Lake Terrace I easily persuaded myself that the shopping reconnaissance could be postponed. The lake was putting on one of its sunny picture postcard days, calm and blue, curving over the southern horizon to the peaks of Tongariro National Park.

A few launches were pottering about and I noticed one of the big commercial vessels idle past the navigation beacon at the mouth of the boat harbour, then lift its bow as it headed out to find trout for the paying guests. Motels on land and motels on water — Stanley would have loved loathing every bit of it. I bought an ice-cream and a meat pie at a snack bar, that being as balanced as I wanted my lunch to be, and sat on the grass verge above the lake in the warm sun. Then I noticed Angela McDonald, Dunkie's sister, the devious matchmaker of my fourth form days.

She was sitting some distance from me eating sandwiches. She was wearing a white smock. Although she was seated with her back to me, I recognized the profile of her face at once when she turned to look at something further down the lake front. I walked over to her and we burst into one of those animated 'it's been so long since I saw you' conversations that jump around like exploding firecrackers as people catch up on what each has been doing since they last met.

Angela had left school at the end of the sixth form, at the same time as Dunkie had left the seventh, and had lived in Auckland where eventually she began a nursing course. I didn't ask too many questions, but I gathered that she had been very unsettled after her brother's death. She had not completed the nursing course, had gone to Australia for a while, failed to find anything worth doing, and made her way back home where her partial qualifications had been enough to land a job at the desk in a doctor's surgery. And here she was having her lunch break in the sun.

There was one subject we had not mentioned, and we both knew it. Angela picked at a blade of grass and was quiet for a moment. Then she said quickly, 'Do you ever think about Duncan?'

'Yes — not as much as I used to — but I still think about him.'

'So do I. That sounds silly — he was my brother. But it's more than that. I don't know how to put it into words. It's just that he was growing up so fast when it happened. He was becoming so different. We'd stopped arguing and - oh, I'm getting so muddled!'

'I know what you mean. You and Dunkie weren't the only ones who were changing.'

Angela glanced at me, smiling. 'That's true.'

'What are you getting at?'

'He told me about that old bloke you worked for. What was his name? Swinton? I asked him why he went up there so often and he said, "I like the hired help."'

I grinned. 'That sounds like me talking.'

'Just what I thought at the time.'

'Dunkie was very interested in Stanley Swinton,' I said reflectively. 'He would have loved what happened afterwards — but, then, if he hadn't died, I doubt if it would have happened at all.' Angela looked very puzzled. 'I was thinking aloud,' I said.

We sat looking at the lake and, to change the subject, I made some comment about how I used to be partly afraid of it because it was so strange and huge. Then she said, 'I'm beginning to think that myself.'

'Why's that?' I asked, expecting some remark about how cold the lake was, or something of the kind.

But she looked at me carefully. 'You promise you won't tell anyone? I'm not supposed to talk about patients.'

'I promise,' I said instantly.

She began slowly. 'Two strange things happened in the same week. It was late last month. Two emergency cases. The first one was a lady. She came into the surgery late one afternoon nearly fainting, with a huge bandage wrapped around one hand. We were flat out at the time, so I went with her into the little operating theatre to look after her until a doctor was available. While we were waiting she told me what happened. It was the strangest thing. She'd been out fishing on the lake with her husband, over Horomatangi Reef. She'd put her hand over the side of the boat, trailing it in the water, when all of a sudden it felt as though her hand had been hit by a club. When she brought it up — I hope you've finished your lunch — when she brought it up, the ends of two fingers were missing!'

(Now where have you heard of something like that before, Robbie? Keep calm, get the facts and react naturally.)

'Good grief,' I said, 'how awful!'

'That's what I thought,' Angela said. 'I'd never heard of anything like it. I mean, a trout wouldn't do that would it?'

'I shouldn't think so,' I said, forcing my eyes wide open in amazement. 'Why was she dangling her hand in the water in the first place?'

'I'm not sure — wait, yes I am. She mentioned that. She'd nicked her finger on a hook when she was changing a fly, and she put her hand in the water to wash the blood away.'

'What did the doctor have to say about it?'

'Oh him! He said that she must have got her fingers caught in the propeller. But, I mean, if you've got your hand over the *side*, you can hardly get it caught in the propeller, can you?'

(Quite so, Angela, but never underestimate the gurus of medicine, law, and God when they set out to explain the inexplicable.)

'What about the other case?'

149

'That was funnier still. It happened just two days later. The whole waiting room heard that one. Tommy Davis wandered in one morning with a bloody looking towel wrapped round his right foot. Have you heard of Tommy?'

'I don't think so.'

'You must be one of the few who hasn't. He's a regular visitor to court. He poaches trout, and he always gets caught, only this time it wasn't a ranger who got him. He reckoned it was an eel.'

'An eel? There aren't any eels in Taupo.'

'Tommy reckons they've just arrived. One of his mates was in the waiting room, just beside the desk, and Tommy told him all about it — and everyone else as well.'

'What happened?'

'Tommy said he was having a look round one of the upper pools in the Waitahanui, which means that Tommy was looking around with a net and probably a fish spear as well. He'd taken his waders off because they were hurting him. He'd sprained his big toe or something, so when he spotted this school of strange looking trout under a bank, he'd waded in with his bare feet to "have a go at them", as he put it. That was as far as he got, because the next thing he knew, he felt something slam into his foot, then a terrific pain in his toe. When he leapt out on to the bank, the toe was gone. Just like that!'

'The sprained toe?'

'I think so. He offered to take the towel off to show his mate, but I wouldn't let him.'

'What did the doctor say about that one?'

'He said Tommy was so boozed half the time, he wouldn't have known how he'd done it.'

'Sounds a really sympathetic bloke, your doctor.'

'One of the old school,' said Angela with a smile.

'Mind you, if what Tommy says is true, it makes you wonder, doesn't it?'

'It certainly does,' I said, nodding wisely.

We said goodbye, promising to get in touch again soon, but both of us knowing that we wouldn't, unless chance made our paths cross. After she had gone I sat thinking for a long time. It was well into the afternoon before I stood up and walked slowly home. I was trying to decide what to do. Whatever the medical profession might think, I *knew*! Stanley's twelve good disciples who had adapted were swimming free, along with their young ones, beginning to spread the word in the cold, watery depths. I wondered whether some lucky person was still making use of the windfall, brand-new chilly bins he had discovered two years before at some deserted spot beside a stream or near the lake. It would be nice to think so. It echoed so well Stanley's yarn about the Rio rubbish collector and the vacuum flasks.

I thought about telling the authorities, more to ease my conscience than anything else, but I knew no one would believe me and I would end up looking silly. I mean, how do you explain someone like Stanley in a few snappy sentences?

('Hello, Mr Policeman, I'd like to report a suspected crime.'

'Really, young lady, how civic-minded of you. Tell me all about it.'

'Well, I once knew this old man called Stanley who used to breed fish — piranha, actually — and I think he might have let some loose in the lake, because I was chatting to someone I know who works in a doctor's surgery and she said they'd had this patient missing a toe, and he reckoned it happened when a couple of fish went for him and...'

'Listen young lady, just leave your name and phone number — don't call us, and we won't call you.')

I cringed at the thought.

That evening I was clearing out some drawers in my room and I came across an old, battered green copy of *A Book of Poetry*. As I leafed through it I read again the pencilled pages of 'Kubla Khan', and I thought it would be a good idea to write it all down, just to let people know what really happened when Taupo's tourist industry discovers that it has a new attraction swimming around in its biggest drawcard — to set the record straight for everyone's sake, but most of all for mine.